THE RED TANK

Also by John Fraser
and published by AESOP Modern Fiction:

Animal Tales
Black Masks
Blue Light / Starting Over
The Case
Down from the Stars
Enterprising Women
Hard Places
An Illusion of Sun
The Magnificent Wurlitzer
Medusa
Military Roads
The Observatory
The Other Shore
Runners
Soft Landing
The Storm
Three Beauties
Wayfaring

THE RED TANK

John Fraser

Aucune guérison n'est retour
à l'innocence biologique

Georges Canguilhem

AESOP Modern Fiction
Oxford

AESOP Modern Fiction
An imprint of AESOP Publications
Martin Noble Editorial / AESOP
28 Abberbury Road, Oxford OX4 4ES, UK
www.aesopbooks.com

First edition published by AESOP Publications

www.johnfraser.info

A catalogue record of this book is available from the British Library.

First edition 2010, revised 2014

ISBN: 978-0-9561409-4-4

Printed and bound in Great Britain by
Lightning Source UK Ltd,
Chapter House, Pitfield, Kiln Farm,
Milton Keynes MK11 3LW

Contents

CHINESE WHISPERS

That heat!
That terrible heat
That coldness!
That terrible coldness

William Carlos Williams

I

HE POKES A LION with his stick, and it runs away. His city is full of conserved beasts, originals but without aggressiveness. Usually. A pact with the mayor. He chooses not to introspect as he goes for his interview.

'... someone to tie on the arms and legs,' says Larry the manager.

'Really, someone else does the tying, and it's better not to anthropomorphise robots,' he – the Engineer, the candidate, me – says.

Larry says, 'Well, I guess it's the movie, and the replicants that die.'

The aspirant, the Engineer, says, 'Stuff that's constructed doesn't die. Your computer gets out of date, it doesn't die. What is no longer there is the idea. Its soul, if you like. It's quite indifferent to its physical shape and fate. It's an idea, surpassed by another idea.'

Larry seems interested: 'So the idea doesn't die

either? Doesn't disappear.'

'Of course not.' The Engineer thinks Larry won't enjoy taking coffee with him in the lounge. Larry asks, 'Where do the ideas come from, if they don't go anywhere?'

'From us, of course. But I think you're strolling up a blind alley.'

Outside they can hear the wild beasts gathered round the fountain, giving tongue. Maybe a murderous scuffle.

I am the Engineer. I don't want the job. Are the robots part of our superorganism, or just appendages because we're lazy? Are robots made in our image or quicker, nimbler, more complicated but quite, quite alien, like our bromided lions? And what if robots reproduce themselves, ever more skilful and neat – sex and procreation's no great invention. And you're free to say, 'how wonderful' or 'how ridiculous'. No one's taking notice.

I get the job. I start to think of moving on.

Larry's wife has been waiting for us – and a bare-knuckle evening. She and Larry must have found each other as two objects interlaced on a beach, washed up but hopeful – Larry wanting a feisty entertainer, and she a predictable patsy with a salary. She comes out swinging, 'Another roboteer! I guess this is the final blow to the workers, cut out their muscles, replace with plastic casings,' and there's Larry, 'We don't have workers, my dear, only women. And if we cut their pay, it's to get their menfolk off their asses and contribute ...'

She says ('by the way, this is my wife, Serena ...') 'You'll open up a bag of tricks, the little buggers, your machines, they don't have sex, don't drink, don't sleep, don't make a mess at home – they'll see you off, you men, and with the knowledge that they'll give you – more idleness, and longer useless lives.'

I say, 'Someone should write a history of sitting down,' but really I'm away, down by those sticky rivers, the men all busy, painting themselves, propitiating gods, maybe plucking a banana. The women somewhere in those sheds, little monkey fingers making knowledge, deep in another culture – and I think, no, that won't do, must start again, and switch off for this evening.

I switch off – he switches off, the evening passes, there are knockdowns, but it's all routine, they'll haggle up to bed, forget me, the non-paying public, then will come another day, inconclusive as the last, but marching on behind no flags.

I repeat the Engineer's mantra, 'Robots can't read a book. Don't know what a problem is – can only scan and solve, they can't invent, think outside their own biscuit tin. So how could they have an idea?'

Serena's unimpressed. 'If you know what an idea is.'

'Yes I do.'

I go on, with my sense of duty, though it's the engineer in me that speaks: 'Robots can iron your pyjamas, sail your ship to Pluto, but they can't make your revolution.'

She says, 'But we don't want that either.'

Lamely, the Engineer says, 'Anyway, one species knows itself. Our dog will give us love, but stays a dog.' I think of our tame lions, what can they give, what, except for tofu slabs, do they take away?

She says, 'And if a robot gives me love, how do I react? You – you seem to me a robot, if you gave me love, what should I expect?'

Well, here we are, all personal, I say, 'I think the best of it lies there – we've no idea, and so the question's back to starters – the robot knows because it's told, how to behave, but as for me – I can behave badly, even carelessly, and that's what makes me engineer and master,' and she sniffs and turns away.

She says, 'Then I think us girls prefer a real robot to an absent male,' and maybe for her it's true.

We sit together on her divan, talking of this and that and neurobiology. Suddenly, with a gesture I can't place at first, she takes off the top half of her clothes, with two handfuls. 'What do you think of me?' she says.

They were just right.

When the Engineer dresses again, thinking perhaps of redress, he asks, 'Larry? Any problems there?'

'Larry doesn't know so many things, one more shouldn't trouble him.'

'You seemed so in synchrony.'

'That's an easy trick.'

I remember my first fantasy realised, my golden girl, down by the river, time unexpected, too unlikely even to be fantasised, then slowly buried under history, becoming merely memory, then fantasy. What became of us? Just archaeology.

And later, Serena says, 'It was good, it didn't matter,' and I think, 'It was so good, it must matter', that's what they say when things are bad.

Serena says, 'Hey, you're off somewhere, becoming engineer again,' and I think of those little complex biscuit tins, all full of pseudo thoughts, philosophy transmuted into silicone, not that the material side concerns me, how they actually make the little buggers after I've designed them, and Serena says,

'Up in the clouds, where thoughts can't reach – you're rather sweet when there's nothing crossing that mind,' and I think that when there's nothing, nothing's all there is, and that's what we're all trying to avoid, that moment when we enter infinity and it all stops – at least, for Serena, up there are clouds and blue.

I – he – presses on relentlessly, 'We can't supply them with God, sex, death or sunsets,' and impatiently she adds,

'Nor reason, love, birth or mountains,' and she laughs, and maybe beneath that surface, itself not so bad, there is another something, good or bad.

She says, 'What I don't see, that puts me with the biscuit tins, is any whole, society, collection of human allsorts – something I'm like and could belong to. Just Larry, and now maybe Larry and you, for how long one doesn't know. A year of Larry on the bottle and we're off, in separate orbits, him to burn up quick and into space waste, me left to wonder what are you? Space dog, so bravely muzzle pointing tail streaming back, or maybe just another piece of beagle shit, spinning round and round ...'

I say, 'No, I'm something live for sure. Some kind of animal. Careless to the fate of others of the species, and so perhaps not one of them. Do not deserve. Invent without a thought for all effects, without a suffering equal to the slightest of the misery of all my brothers. And my sisters too,' and she sees me drifting away from what she wants – her lack, her longing, mild ache for companionship maybe. But not an ache for me. That's yet to come and will make us hop, and poor old Larry too if we make him lose his innocence, what will he take of us – and am I not too far ahead? Serena doesn't want an end game before it's started, wants a slow slow burn. A robot only has its options, like her, a finity of choices.

Of course, I knew I was frittering away my life – the

lives of school friends surfaced, like timbers coming off a wreck, became public, or at least as currency – and money was there too, or status, photos of some bunch of guys, who'd won a cup or signed a peace or merged with some other bank. It all passed by me, and I was as proud and idle as a pyramid in the sand, waiting for robbers of my – maybe stolen – jewels.

And while he chatters on, Engineer Harley has a vision – one of the throwback visions, like a lizard's dreams of fire and brimstone – a past so horrible and immediate, its passage gives, if not rebirth, at least another chance. The parade of shabby dwarves, families of them, the women smaller, children smaller still, all looking straight ahead, avoiding jeers or exploitation, as useful freaks or sports of God. The beggars, and the ragged band, in single file, a chant from hell for who knows what confraternity or leperhouse. And then the feast – a whale, larger than the largest lifesize, patterned in what seemed yellow plastic, or like liner luggage of the Thirties, and so the beast was fake, though starting now to reek, and out come yellow packages, out from its manufactured belly – baby tiger, baby whale. And then the crowd, from all around me, they've all brought some things to hack with, gobble down the risky flesh – advancing on it with a roar like turkeys in a storm, all busy with their mouths to satisfy or howl for some or more. A vision of the past that makes a mock of all the idylls of the riverbank, the sacred tombs are all a load of rot, the gods, the face paint, stories by the fire – all petty tricks to keep the early deaths at bay, a respite from the brother hacking at you, enemies at every tree, the sunny glades are full of killers.

And then he thinks, this fine young engineer, adultery proudly in his stride, his fear is time. Not ageing, as he's young, just time, dimension to be somehow filled, avoiding the unmeaning of its being simply past. It's time as meaning that assails him. Dimension that his robots cheerfully ignore – they do their job, if asked, and if their time runs out, then onward with another! They do not care, because they do not tell the time, their time. Though it's built in, and they are on the forward rush of obsolescence, maybe it's time we can't convince them of, make them evaluate, and savour as it rushes past and reappears, the sea, the sea, always beginning over and the same.

I pull myself back, and Larry's talking of ideas, or his Idea. I say, 'You want me to make robot intellectuals, then? All sitting in a row on shelves, those biscuit tins all staring out the window, interviewing each other, reviewing each others' circuits, – then maybe smoke a pipe, screw a friend's wife, go to a movie?'

'Something like that,' he says, and seems a little disappointed.

'That's how it is,' I tell him, 'Ideas we recognise after the fact – otherwise it's just the brain doodling with itself, joining up the scraps, it's boring, dross. All out of focus, wrong and trivial, and then ...'

'That "then" is what I want,' he says.

'The then, or zen – depends on other people and their wants or fantasies. Those tins can't evaluate each other – and they have no needs, no fantasies.'

And Larry says, 'So, give them what they need to have. Factor it in.'

I say, although I'm keen, 'I doubt myself.'

'It doesn't look like it,' he says.

*

Larry says, 'Engineer Harley!' The call to order.

And I wonder if I've not been somewhat of a shit – but then, we don't own each other any more, although the money keeps on getting counted, and besides, I don't know enough of him, nor of Serena, to say if they are even bigger shits. And in the end, I put it all away, and really I don't feel a thing, and Larry says,

'We've got the biggest challenge for you – you're so big on your ideas: we want you to put them into robots. Not to make them human, nor anything like that, but just ideas. Make them robots with ideas, no science fiction crap about them being warriors or hostile to us. Just let them have ideas.'

He's caught me there.

I say, 'When you try a thing like that, you follow all the same old paths, it all ends up as options and solutions. We don't know how ...' But then I think, 'It's easier to take some kids, put them in clothes and clean them up and cure their bodies, have them read and write – they'll give you all the ideas, quite cheap,' and Larry reads my thought and says,

'If we take humans, if we take the poor ones, their ideas will not be science fiction, but there's a chance that they'll be warriors or hostile to us' and I'm sure that Larry in his modest way is just as big a shit as me.

There's no more intellectuals like Larry wants. Not in our woods, anyway. In France, in China. Or on the Web somewhere, anonymous, pseudonymous. They're beasts of fable anyway.

I poke at two lions with a stick. They run away. They're not a metaphor for whatever Larry wants, inventors, magicians, designers – good old Renaissance men, who'd build a battleship and make a mustard pot – all before lunch, then maybe kill a guy in some alleyway. And I wonder if Larry'd have a try at killing me, Serena being his province, his stab at some significance, and now – well, what? She's hardly compromised, and gesturing's her mark of independence. Independent from him, but only if he knows. I think of robots and their knowledge – they can have none, either of the future or the past. So how can they construct what we call ideas?

We're good together, me and Serena, on that red divan, like in a picture. Seen from above – who by? Some painter, slung up in a hammock, dripping down his paints, righting perspectives, my bottom and her face and vice versa, what fantasy, and how banal. 'Poseurs on an orange sofa' – you do it orange, so it seems a lighter red, and not so permanent, weighty. And you'll see, the story's in the colour – there's the idea: – you'd never teach it to a biscuit tin, for they're just full of biscuits – when empty, then away they go, down to the dump.

I tell him, 'Larry, if there's no tradition, culture, history, the ideas will be the global unrooted ones.'

To myself, I think, *if there are any.*

He says, 'You mean, no overarching intellectuals, just experts or gurus.'

'Of which we have a good helping – critics and lickspittles, as you will.'

He looks awkward. 'Well, Harley, really I had in mind something a little different. A break with tradition. But the founding of a new one.'

'Sounds like more gurus.'

He says, 'What I want is authority plus performance. Not rhetoric and exhortation, but the say and then the do.'

'You want God in a box.'

He hesitates, then, 'What I'd like is something that predicts the earthquake, then makes the guys evacuate – or stops the quake. No shallying around.'

I say, 'Yes, that's God all right. And you want to be Creator of the Creator?'

'No, no. The thing would have free will, and you, Designer, a percentage.'

I smile. 'That's your intelligent design. I'm flattered you imagine I could handle it. We may have to spin off another moon to fit in all the bits.'

'Well, what would you need to start?'

'The backs of lots of envelopes.' And I think, who is madder, the prime creator or His designer, but Larry says, 'And it's big bucks too.'

I say, 'I'll get by on my salary,' and he jumps in, 'Maybe you want a model, for the ethical side. I know a man of substance – well, not substance in cash terms, rather – of principle. A guy not like us, free floaters, quite carefree except for expenditures and cancer scares, but really anchored, full of principle. Worthy of respect.' He is magnificent. He adds, 'And not a word about all this, you know, to Serena.'

We never hear again of this munificent ghost, Larry's fixer, sharer in the honours, bearer of the losses, but now I have to say:

'Of course not, nothing to Serena. Bring this avatar forward, please.'

It seems to me that first I must discard the faith-and-patience religions. The more temples, monks and priests, and savvy elders and encyclicals and funny rules and diets, sex on Thursdays, kill the girlchild but spare the cockroach – all that just won't compute. All the big religions, the monotheistic and the spiritual ones, they're all attached to faith-and-patience – accept what happens as the best, follow the rules, keep on believing, don't expect a lot, and if it happens and is bad, as it will be, just take it in your stride, or wherever else is possible. No, that's not what we want – we need analysis and then decisive action. I can see a long journey'll be required, to see how the effective operators produce results and keep the clients – if not happy, then alive.

The Engineer gets up early, leaves his building. He's convinced a new creation, layered on the old attempt, is beyond his, or anyone else's powers. But he has hopes – not faith – that he'll find something worthwhile, maybe the shamans, maybe Confucius, or Dao. Even some lay, quite earthy, ideology, to give the key to this world – and he smiles as he thinks that Larry's remit includes paradise, and then he thinks what he'll do about Serena, and decides to let things carry him along.

He carries his long stick. He sees among the shrubs four, or even five, young lions, taking their ease or looking happy. He's about to give a warning poke with his long stick, and then – a cop springs out from behind a tree.

'Hey, you, just leave those animals alone!'

'Just a precaution. Because you never know.'

'They've the same right as you. Leave them be.'

'Just to establish a distance.'

'Give me that stick!'

They tussle, quite politely, on the Engineer's part there is a little fear, or apprehension, the cop is thinking of the threats allowed or just permitted during a resistance, and the Engineer lets go, and says, 'On your head, then. I hope they're as civilised as we,' and the cop talks of unprovoked assault and suchlike, but for both of them the day has started with a little resolution of an obstacle, the lions lope off, the traffic stops to let them cross the road and seek a fountain.

He is disturbed by the affair of the stick, but slowly returns into himself. He, no, I think about miracles. If you do the miracle without a situation to precede it, then it will seem a trick, entertaining but futile. If you let the presidents and all that political stuff define a problem for you, which you then resolve, the politicians take the credit and fish you in. The only way is find the situation, then resolve it, all by yourself. Not an easy reading of the landscape – for the situation must be imminent – a fire, a meteorite, an epidemic. Not an academic puzzle, tests and debates.

I stare out of the window. Some cops with a truck are shifting a hippo from the fountain. They're using sticks and what seem guns with darts. They pepper the beast, who's shackled. It falls, its little paws pedal bravely, it sleeps, it dies. We all think of our own, our multidoctored deaths, we sympathise, we turn away, it is the sadness of the world. The truck backs up, the meat is hoisted in with hooks and pulleys. Peace is back, the cops are sharing beers, it's hot, of course.

I think about miracles.

I think about Serena. There's a situation. No need to be cautious, maybe. Throw away the stick. Although – one never knows.

*

Next time, Serena greets me, 'I must be mad, letting another mad scientist into my life.'

'I didn't know I was in your life,' I say.

She doesn't respond. She talks about the lions. 'There's lots of people I could see eaten up.'

'Better to withdraw than get involved with feline rights,' I say.

'Well no, I guess – where'd we be without other people?'

'Our robots don't seem to have that need.'

'I bet when you're not around, they're all real chatter-boxes!' she says.

It's a daunting thought. And as we get together, in what the Engineer thinks a peculiar form of gymnastics – only apparently more gratifying than most – jumping the horse, the bars, the rings – maybe they all started off as sex games, now detached, autonomous, and all of us just carrying out our tasks, each task separated from the next – like work from play – and then when it's done each person separating from their mate, and leaning back on that divan, she says, 'Larry's got some big ideas.'

'I'm not Larry,' I say. 'Anyone can have them, even cosmic, talking to the spirits, addressing nature, all that stuff. It's part of our vainglory.' I see she savours that word, a wild card not in any of the hands she's dealt herself.

Serena says, 'You in your small world. Me in mine. Does this … this sex stuff, bring us together?'

I think for a while. 'People say so. And besides, my world isn't tiny, it's immense. It's just that everything is dead. Or rather, everything goes about its business, and we'd like to think – predictably, automatically, according to its rules. But it's limitless – for practical purposes.'

She persists, 'Why don't you do brains. Or kittens.'

'I do brains too, up to a point. But it's all systems, where kittens have a cultural baggage, they cry when they're being hurt.'

She ponders. 'Like Larry. But then, in marriage you both know that in the best case you'll have to care for some old wreck when you least feel like it – or when you want to be off on a cruise.'

I comfort her, 'Larry can't be more than fifty.'

'He's thirty-five. But has the ideas of someone grasping for eternity. Into the brain of God, he says.'

'I thought God had stopped tweaking the universe, left it all to run, the tweakers are just us.'

She objects. 'It's all a puzzle, and when guys like Larry look for meanings behind the wallpaper, they come up with exercise and dahlias.'

'And young therapists,' I say, trying to do Larry a good turn, find him another exit.

'Well,' she says, 'Maybe I'll be your single living thing, in all your immensity. It doesn't flatter me, but it gives you something to play with.'

*

She says, 'Maybe we can populate the spheres,' and laughs.

'You mean, after death?'

'You, me, Larry, motoring in his Mustang round Orion's Beltway?'

'We'd find it difficult, without brains.'

She laughs, 'That's how he drives anyway. So, why don't you try to fill up all that emptiness? Try Pascal, Proust, Schopenhauer ...'

I say, 'You're just firing them off like rockets? Anyway, it's not really empty. Just daunting. Not even silent, but not what you'd call musical.'

She thinks a moment. 'So there aren't aliens – it's just the whole extent that's alien?'

'Nicely put.' She's trying to make a contact with me. I acknowledge it. I say, 'You know what Larry wants me to do for him?'

'Find something out there, but no spaceships. Find something to establish his name forever, but not just on a piece of rock up there. Find something that makes him feel powerful.'

I say, 'The last of these, for sure. And all done from my desk.' Then, graceless, 'I should be going now. And I've lost my stick.'

'Never worry, Engineer. Nature's been quite tamed out there. The fields to feed us, rivers to light our lamps, all the animals at risk are gathered in the city bounds,' she laughs, a little wistfully.

I say, 'Well, I'm not so trusting as you.'

'A little bit of life,' she says, 'won't do you harm.'

I say that I agree, though being beaten up – or eaten – isn't in my scheme.

She clings patiently to me: 'Don't be concerned for Larry. All he wants is power and then an easy death. Power into money too, but not so much, it's all a symbol. He wants to plan, be grandiose and brash, and that's enough. He isn't stupid, Harley. He sets a task impossible, but the fruits are his.'

'OK,' I say, 'but what's success for him is bound to be my failure. What he wants just can't be done – a box of stuff that must convince the world, the public, that it represents the latest trick in spirituality. And – suppose we start the earthquake, and can't stop it, shakes us all to bits?'

'Well,' she says, 'Don't expect me to help you glue it

all together. And for the genie in the bottle – it's all ephemeral, it's argument, there's no hard corners, no dawns or sunsets. No divan.'

And as I leave, casting an eye for lions and such, I wonder that she's so convinced the divan is the centre, and I glance up, at that monstrous sky, that seems a bowl but really is just light and rock, and sounds like string quartets played backward, it's just an awful puzzle that if you solve it leaves you as you were. Though maybe with a medal.

The Engineer thinks – for he is not stupid, for he is not without some culture...

He thinks, I think, 'What does Larry want me to slide into those interstellar spaces – man, God? From the canyons? Hölderlin's dreams from the asylum? A public all empowered, all of us clotted with our histories, embracing the feminine, our past and present slaveries? The harmonies of nothing, of the dust rubbing against dust?' The Engineer thinks, I think, of Serena – can the answer to all this be sexual intercourse? Why, surely not. Serena on her goddess throne, a lotus in her hand and at her feet a lion couchant.

The Engineer resumes his work, it's so familiar, all the thoughts he must put in, the eventualities in what he calls the biscuit tins, that cure – what? Curiosity, perhaps. The drive to power that's based on error and inevitable failure. Try to convince me, I think, but I'll not be convinced. They say that is the most human thing, and necessary, the scepticism that gets you up each morning, another day – the sun, the sun, the chariot pulled by four lions, that sweeps the stars below, gives us the illusion that the sky is just a dome with one hotspot. That could make you weep. Who is fooled? Why, no one, that's why we go on.

*

I – the Engineer – go to a conference. It's mostly about brains. We all take good care, or manage close surveillance, of our brains. Some jog, some don't eat, or sleep, some drink only bourbon, lots of it. There are clumps of leaders, looking like Larry, each clinging to their foothold on the mountain. Doctors young and doctors grey, funded and busted, doctors randy, doctors virginal. But between us all a power of computation nearly equal to one laptop's.

Each brings out a piece of study – it's like a dog show, walking each around. Different races – no one says they're only interested in the big ones.

Two guys from the village are brought up, to give a little concert – Henze's Auden songs, I think – and we all nod through.

And everyone has heard of Larry's plan, they're interested but bemused. It's what we'd all like to do, and know we can't. Know it can't be done. It's making gold with spells – there's not one here who, if you did it, wouldn't take an ingot home.

A lady doctor's here, she faces up to me as though I'm fearsome. In China things to do with brains are pressing. She says, 'I think that what you or your boss proposes is – making disaster, then reversing it, or making it benign. You want to prove a miracle has taken place – it's one you've staged, in other words, a con.'

I think that's so, besides, the risks are dire. There's lots of us who do real things, with bombs and mountains, all those tests, the systems working out like hamsters – but stage a disaster not by accident – that's a risk we just don't run.

I say, 'Really, the important bit is mapping spaces,' but she's not convinced. 'To do the risky things,' she says, 'you need a Party, all the rest won't cover for you. Experiment in white coats has its frontiers, but to convince, to sway the world – Party's the thing.'

She opens up a road that I'll not travel. Not being the convincing type myself, and Larry's just a boss. Maybe she's right – to me it's just a tawdry trick, banal, making an error, turning insides out, then change the tune – it's hardly what we want. But what we want is grandiose, but also – it's banal. Even the respect of all these guys, from every place – they're just like me, a brain on legs, endlessly replicated, endlessly begun again. Is this the treasure of the world? I guess it is, the Engineer guesses it is so. But can I kneel before myself, my brothers, likenesses?

I stand alone, high above the sea wrinkled, with dhows whose white sails are like the folded wings of doves, pecking and contemplating. The ground is umber, quite higgledy-piggledy, rising in big clods, some broken plants that look like cannabis. It is terribly hot, I feel I'm in a glass dome, a dome of molten glass. Then I see I'm in a Muslim cemetery, the souls all flown, the headstones half deflated, some lying down, their standing days done. The signs of life are far below, though you wouldn't say it's human, but there's movement.

This cemetery beside the sea – it doesn't chime with death, just this hot day, and not quite liveliness but 'far away'. Snakes – there'll be snakes, and I of course without my stick. I think of all the predecessors, who spent their days musing in places such as this, and drew a whole lesson, a whole text, from contemplating.

The Chinese delegate comes up to me. She says, 'Somewhere below, I saw a circle of women dancing – no, not from here, I think they're Kosovars, and some were in the ancient clothes and some in modern, and there's three guys, two with those old clarinets that squeal like boars on heat and someone with a shaman's drum – all going at it, at the dance. Such joy!'

I say primly, 'Surely they're not delegates? From the conference, you want to be alone,' and she says, 'Ah yes, but you'll have heard last night, in the hotel, what farce! The corridors, the doors and what else exchanged, some, yes, for the academic stuff, some for the booze, but others – for the pleasures of their company.'

'It doesn't bother me.'

'It isn't a bother for anyone. But think, we're all here to say how close we are to a revelation, latest secrets of the cosmos ...'

I say, primly again, 'When you take the universe and boil it, chill it, tape it, probe it, speed it up and slow it down, and measure it and put your toe over its threshhold – yes, if you call the unknown "secret", secrets revealed there are. But what's the use of secrets when they aren't secret any more? You hang your name on the discovery – then you're up here, the cemetery by the sea.'

She's unconvinced. 'We're not so far along, it's true. The link between the action and the thought. That's not a natural trip, it's all against nature. Maybe we could collaborate?'

I say defensively, 'I don't see how. I think I'm up a dead end. And besides, I've got a girlfriend,' and I think of Serena, and the Chinese doctor says, 'And where's she from, is she Italian, they say that they're the best,' and I reply, 'I haven't asked her, but I don't think there's any rule in this,' but after all, why not collaborate, give oneself over, say yes I will, yes, forget this cemetery, the wrinkled sea, just do what comes. 'When we have boiled the sea,' I say, 'we have its secret, but the rest is not a secret, all the rest is difference. Interpretation.'

But she won't let me go, I say, 'You understand, I'm not attractive as a person,' and she, 'I'm interested in your mind, and not your body. Rather, the thought, that drives your robots, then maybe—'

'I really can't collaborate, it's all too vague,' and I think, 'She wants to steal my stuff,' and then, 'So, if it goes to China, why should I care? It's not made to be a profit for mankind,' and then I think, 'Maybe it is.'

She says, 'To fill the universe with thought's a noble thing,' and I say, 'Fill it up with junk, you mean,' but she continues, 'That is, yes, noble, if a little crass. Might even be of use – the other thing is horrible. To make disasters then reverse their effects, for self-aggrandisement – no, that's not on.'

She's right. No more 'yes I will', I say, 'No, I won't.' And screw Larry. Maybe I'll depart, depart with Serena, who I've never seen, not really seen away from the divan, and is that urge so strong it means to change a life, or even two, if she would come, and where, and how? And who would pay?

'You're not so bad a person, after all,' says the Chinese doctor, and looks coyly, 'But I mean to steal your thoughts,' and I suppose she means it as a complement, or just a threat to have me follow her, but why, my thoughts are not the kind that lead to action – rather, they lead me back to Larry.

And she's gone, back to the Kosovars who're having whatever fun they can, and who knows why they're here, as maybe delegates or perhaps they sweep the hotel corridors, and why's the Chinese lady here, except for routine, who knows what she builds, it could be rockets or the management of infants, making of catflaps or of prison doors – the things we have to do but rather not to think about, and have we come to this, and then I think, to come to this from what before – and then I think that really in my mind there isn't a 'before', or surely not a golden one, relations breaking off or not begun, the lives all zeroing to cemeteries like this, and maybe some crude images – of people, adulterers even, being hanged from cranes or starving in tin shacks.

I say to the Chinese doctor, 'When we think of thought, we start from a grey mass of writhing, horrible things, impulse and wishful thinking, and the deeds that tell us only that we can repeat them, and we will, to end up here. This goddam heat, and bits of worn-out body, look at the dogs that come up here, poor goddam things they're hungry, but a bone's a bone, and no one cares, why should they, these old rags and shreds don't mean a thing,' and I go on inside, and Serena and her Schopenhauer, they all stand bold and free, beyond my reach or comprehension, up in the sky like stars, who'd want to go there, who would want to shout, 'Yes, I'll go there,' and I realise that lots of delegates would hop into that capsule, maybe a robot'd do it all instead, and whizz up to some notional planet, find a piece of ice, maybe a lily maybe not, and bring it back, a thousand years from now – and straight into this heap of earth. And if I stage a miracle, a real one, who will care? What lesson is there?

The Chinese doctor says, 'The trick will be to keep on doing them, then to remedy disasters that you haven't thought of, haven't planned, and can't redress,' and I think, 'Yes that's one big flaw! By that time, Larry'll be dead and famous, and we'll be in that trek, from schism to a heresy, more massacred, more doctors, human condition and all that,' and she takes my hand, and that is that, probably she thinks, 'Another mad one, poor guy, out in space beyond the rope to pull him back in with the rest of us,' and I think, 'Maybe I did wrong to talk the walk, to leave the capsule, venture off, and walk on nothing all alone', the sea is far below, the sun is cracking hot, the sound of ancient clarinets leaks up to us – I let her lead me down, the poor old blind man, who knows what he's done up there, incest and murder for a start – but when we're back on earth I see that all the other guys – some with their avatars and some with new-found mistresses, are all strolling round as if they're blind or drunk, and one, a stranger, says to me, 'Too goddam hot to think of anything, we go inside, there'll be another concert, more traffic in the corridors by night, and nothing more to think this day.'

*

Serena asks, 'How was the conference?'

'I met a Chinese girl. There were two tiny concerts. We saw some Kosovars. No one seemed to think Larry's up to much.'

She says, primly, 'I'm still Larry's girl, you know. What did they play?'

'First some Henze, I think it was. Auden songs, for the mood. Then the second night, some Gil Evans, a group of replicants, they did Time of the Barracudas.'

'Quite apt. And did you and the Chinese make the music of the spheres?'

'She wants to steal my stuff. If there is any. She asked if you were Italian.'

'My name perhaps, but not the thought behind it. Quite classy music, though.'

'Just some local lads. And lots of brains walking around – and I saw a Muslim cemetery, high above the sea. The day was hot as lead, molten lead. Or glass.'

She asks again, 'No problem, then?'

'Slight apprehension about snakes. That plan to outdo the gods, enact the second coming, miracles – that seemed to stall. I decided not to set off volcanoes – not quite ethical. And a bit inconclusive too.'

She says, 'If you're afraid of lions, you're probably afraid of volcanoes too.'

Unexpected, Larry arrives. I'm sitting on the divan, heavy with – well, not guilt, but not wanting to be caught, for sure.

We talk, I say to Larry, 'That task, all power to the boss – you know – it's best not to talk too much about it.'

'The talking's the best part, gets you in the frame. Besides, I do it all for Serena. I feel she doesn't respect me,' he kids, and she kittens up to him.

He continues, 'The idea goes on, OK, I've not backed out. Just let's kick it around a little more.'

It seems to me, yes, that's what we'll do – it's like those equations waiting to be solved, you get a million bucks you don't know what to do with, except give them back – with your name on them. Not at all the plan we started. I put it back, high on a shelf in my mind, where it can't escape.

I think, 'How terrible to have no fear, save of a natural death. Not that death's so natural these days. That's all Larry wants – immortality at 35. But no fear, fear of some species member. Larry's all against nature. He doesn't see the young goddesses of death that walk among us,' and I think of the young Chinese girl, who wants. Not wants of me, just wants, longs – for knowledge, I suppose. Unlike Larry. And unlike me – I'm scared of it. What a weight! Where is it supposed to end? More real than we have now, or less enchanted? Philosophy for the stars, but with a sucker punch to come.

If Larry can't be lord of the universe, well, there's always Serena. For him, or me. I rather hope for me. I hope. Maybe.

II

NO LIONS. No lions at the door this morning. It's like the first day at school, knowing that by midday, as you've been promised, you'll come home knowing everything. And had a good time, too. The Engineer has to meet up with Larry. I have to.

He says, 'We screwed up with the last project.'

'It wasn't so stupid. Just didn't show what it should, what we thought.'

'Well,' he says, 'Putting different things together, that's what the game is, that's what café tables are for.'

'I suppose so.'

He asks, and I tell him, 'There was a Chinese girl at the conference. Does she want to help, or steal?'

Larry laughs, 'Science is all made up of that. The decisive move is not the solution, it's the layout of the problem.'

'Some people let it happen. Or watch it happening.'

The Engineer thinks of Serena, and watching it happening.

Larry says, 'Of course, you can't plan for innovation,' but of course you do.

'You see this glass, on this table,' he goes on. 'This woman on this divan. And what do you need to sweep them into your design?'

The Engineer, I, think, 'Nothing, you need nothing, not even a design!

Larry goes on: 'To leap from that mind, your mind – to something larger. To make the leap, make the contact – identify the larger thing. Nature, the animals, it's wrong, too cluttered, too improvised, a dictionary. You need a field of action, field of being, where you're significant, where your experience links in a wider field of thinking but where action plays its part. You see, Harley?'

I think, 'mind into Mind?' and say, 'The thought-out life? Lived well, largely foretold? Perhaps an engineer's job, but then – the world's all set up already. There's nothing left to do. There is the glass, the table, woman and divan. But where do I come in? Drink from the glass, make love to, even love, the woman?' I didn't use the rougher words that came to mind – and after all, Serena'd thrown her dice, knew it could come down light.

'Maybe you could make a die with one face zero,' I say, but he can't follow me.

He says, 'At this point, it's attribution, that's what counts. Yes, nothing can be other, there it is – what matters is that this whole scene appears, is attributable,' he presses down the word, 'to us. To me. Signed, with my name. That's the thing that counts – not changing – naming. Though I could cut you in, percentage wise.'

While the Engineer, the – my – voice of reason, listens to Larry, running wild through fields of fame and power, I listen to a radio Larry keeps always on, as others might a coffee pot or bottle, occupying another lobe of his immense brain. There's a guy there, saying, 'Long-legs, the boss, he'd no truck with unions, nor with written contracts; we was black from Kentucky up into Idaho, we played the bars, picked up a stripper at the bus stop when we come in, and then we all, we five, we holed up in some hotel and had, you get me, something to drink and if they had it, something stronger, then we walked out like warriors with a train of booty – looking for a patch to call our own, maybe a Thursday to a Sunday morn, and hardly saw the sun come up, go down, the guys were coming in off shift and supping up and when we'd done, say round two o'clock there's always someone with a place, even a forest or a parking lot where we could play on and on, and maybe they could even pirate us, and sell some tapes or make a disc or two, we never knew, – then on the bus, and all as black as black, no one else would ever play with us, the bars were blacked and goddam all our eyes the barmen said, and so they went black for months or years, it wasn't really fair, but we got paid a lot in kind and guys would give us rides and beds and drink and stuff, even a shirt and pants, and so it was playing in the warm, we did our whole works, and even them, the ballerinas, how'd they ever strip to jazz quintet but we was blowing hard and really didn't care, the flesh was twirling round somewhere and smoke was coming from the horns and battering at the skins and Longlegs trumpeted like the mouths of hell, and call it blues or what you like, and it was sad and goofy as it came to us, and colours black and grey and brown as coconuts or polished wood, the guys just drank it up and made their lives if not a heaven then a hell more interesting till one night a guy give us a ride and was so drunk he spun us off and maybe we got hit before or after and all of us all intertwined and blood and glass and feathers, all that stuff and claws and maybe we had hit a forest, goddam birds and foxes how she squawked the stripper, said "Swing in that golden sky you chariot, you silly slave" and we was all just busted up and uninsured and high and drunk and half asleep…' There was a long laughter, and the musician ends, 'And so I went out West, arranger, death with glory, not another goddam note did pass my lips,' more laughter.

And I want to fill a huge room with sound, and Larry says, 'I've my impulsive side, you know, Harley now – you're a pretty level chap that's how we get to where we got, I know I can rely on you, but me, you know, I got Serena who's real class and tranquil, but I guess I'm always searching, looking for the next. You'll find it too – stasis is dull,' the radio laughs on.

Larry is still talking, '... and so the real money I banked, the fairy money I gave to everyone else. They were really happy in fairyland, and maybe when that one disappeared there's another waiting. And you're just the figure on my nuptial cake, young Harley, the link between greed and power,' and he laughs.

I say, 'I'm the oil in your skullpan, then? And Serena?'

'She's in distribution. They pay her in free time.'

I say, 'Seems a bit imprecise.'

'That's what I say, she shouldn't mix business with leisure!' Again he laughs, and I ask, 'Larry, is it really business that we're in? You seem long past that kind of thing.'

He looks out the window. Below there are animals wandering round, waiting for the next feed, and he waves a hand, 'Well, I can't fix the climate, if we want it fixed – so I can try to give the guys some sense of meaning – Harley, we're the fire ants of creation – we don't do sorry, or "slow down" – down with the old and gobble up the new, it's how we're made, it's how we got our brains' and he taps his skullpan. 'It's like Serena does, when she gets a question she can't answer, goes "gobble gobble", turkey eats, turkey gets ate, what turkey know, turkey can't escape.'

I agree, though I've never thought about it, 'Speed stealing...'

'Forget past slights, past wrongs,' he says, 'for sure you've had them done, maybe you'll do them. Just not a feature.'

I think of that loud music, bars like barns, us animals all shrieking, screwing in the corners, then on the tables, kids running in and out. The only thing is music, loud as you can – better to play it than to listen to it, goddam derivative racket, all bum notes, polished with love, those plummy melodies – but if you can, up there with your instrument, shooting it out. The stuff of life.

Not one of the sad guys getting deafened – pilgrim a musician be! Play it out!

I think of the Chinese girl, of those poor Kosovars, dancing in some highway layby, and I think again, maybe they're not so poor, and what hell is patterned with the Chinese girl, all fancy fantasy, bodies unknowing sliding into orbit.

Suddenly, Larry asks, 'Do you ever feel remorse, Harley.'

'I don't think so.'

But it seems he really wants to know what it is, what it does.

I think, 'Is this about Serena, she is her own, Serena's girl, not Larry's and not mine, and indeed, she's for herself – like all the rest, which rather lets us out.'

'If you lead people what you think's astray,' Larry says, 'and do them bad, you're only sorry if you know something – about them, about you, the universe, and so and so. So, really remorse is about knowing more. The more you know, the more remorse, but if you're ignorant, you can do just about anything, and so the doing's not the problem, it's just what you know, or maybe how you know it, so it's not the bad things you come to recognise, it's just the kind of knowing that you have,' and he presses on, and I wonder what the hell he did, and he concludes, 'And so, you do some good things and your knowledge comes that really they were bad, you feel remorse – and wish? What, you'd never done the things that you thought good? Or wish you didn't feel remorse, because you didn't know? Or now you think you know, and you feel bad, but maybe you put another layer down, and so you're not so sure – it's slippery, Harley.'

'That's why I keep you, Harley,' he says, after a pause. 'Give me knowledge, but all the same, no remorse.'

'All I do is tell you what's impossible,' I say.

'Yes, everything I've done was impossible,' he muses. 'Everything I want to do, you tell me is impossible.'

Maybe he wants another engineer to tell him what's impossible, I think, but if he fires me, what do I lose? A life ascetic, up will come another one, still more ascetic, but be shot of him, new doors to fairylands all new and fragrant, but I'll then know so much, the guys who're really poor, their brains all withered on the stalk – yes, they do useless, vicious things, and I can judge them so, but me ...' I'm pretty smug, I realise. And that's another thing to know.

'I tell you quick and clean what is impossible,' I say.

He nods, and rears up to his height, tycoon or minor god, who cares.

*

'What can Larry have done, that he wants to feel remorse?' I ask Serena.

'Slavery,' she says.

'Any particular kind? Wage slavery, relationships, trafficking? Or just bound to wheels of time and place?'

She waves her legs in the air, 'Can't you see my slave bracelets, or are they chains?'

I say, 'We're all against it and it's all around us – free people who pay for trips on the slave ships, slaves through the identities they've chosen, runaways living in the forests of their documents. But all tycoons like slaves, and when those run, they just buy others,'

'Larry has the will to enslavement, like his friends,' Serena says.

'Larry has friends?' I say, surprised.

'It's part of being rich. Modern rich, that is.'

'But if slave-owning's part of being rich – forget the friends – why should he feel remorse?'

'I don't think he does, it's just his whim, that way he feels more human.'

'But he already is … more human than the rest of us. He says that everything he's ever done has been impossible – and look how the people love him for it.'

'For all the rest of us,' she says, 'our freedom, independence, what could it be? Like finding in old age that you're autistic, never managed to make it to the selling block.'

'It all seems very vague, and metaphorical,' I tell her. 'I don't see him owning slaves, it's too responsible, a cluttered role, and suffering that brings no joy to anyone.'

'Not owning, silly!' she says. 'Buying and selling. Things. Stuff. The slavery's in his interests, not his accounts. But that remorse – is strange. It's all part of the system.'

'Something extra,' I say, not very wise or interested.

And Serena catches at the phrase, interprets it her way.

'This physical stuff,' I say, when we have separated our bodies, and I know it's a dangerous moment and a dangerous thing to say, 'It doesn't seem to mean so much. What does it say?'

'What did your Chinese girl, sorry, your colleague, rival, inspiration, what does she mean?'

'Nothing original to say, said in an original way.'

'So, that's the physical. Better this than the police car, cattle truck, tented hell, taser and billy, tumour and blindness.'

I say, 'I guess you're right. But – I'm a heretic, you know – our job is all about the solving, solving ancient problems and the new ones, neatest answer wins the prize. But to me, the beauty's in the problem.'

'Now,' she says, shaking herself down, 'That is perverse. Really perverse.'

I look to see if that's a joke. She says, 'That's Larry's secret. The impenetrable. It isn't really secret, because he knows it, and he always acts on it, impossible things are just the forest where he gets his firewood. Man with an axe, a green man bowed under fresh branches. That's Larry.'

I wonder, is it a good thing that we are close to him, and, therefore, close to each other, and so fugitives, till the moment when splitting from each other is the best hope, one at least may make it to a shelter. Other Larrys. And yet – being owned by Larry doesn't hurt, he is the Master, and he acts, he doesn't know we know, and what we do is freetime, is what we do just for ourselves. He'll never see the Kosovars, dancing by the sea. Maybe Serena's part of this bondage business, I think. Maybe she's not into caprice but conspiracy? Is she part of Larry's bargain, or revolt against him?

She says, 'Larry's a facilitator. Likes to have us round him, and bound to him – but so's he can get shot of us. Then there's the favours, done for friends – supplies of labour. And of horses, dogs, and women, even other human types, and animals – it all abounds with him. Nothing direct, but so the wheels go round, and at the bottom real slaves – not just those that come in ships and trucks, but those who can't get out, locked into factory and warehouse, field and farm ...'

'Usually when people are as rich as Larry, others do the favours for them,' I say.

'He's too good-hearted,' she says.

The laws are all arithmetic, I think, and we're not at the centre of anyone's concerns. 'It all rolls on,' I say, 'bit more, bit less, the two steps forward, then two back – the rhythm of our dance. Behind one Larry, others wait, who can refuse a favour, something that makes us humans differ from our friends outside,' and from the window I see wild beasts lurching about, trying to copulate, but short on fantasy.

She says, 'It's so. But Larry can't just be our end, our goal, our puppet master,' and I think 'His vision, his impossible tasks, those give me life, form horizons,' and then I think, I don't know why, about the Chinese girl, what's she doing in my head, where'll I lead her or be led?

'I find these animals,' I say, 'wandering about, thinking what to do, what they are, quite irritating,'

'Like us, but they say more beautiful,' Serena says,

though she's not convinced, and maybe thinks of mathematics, which they say is beautiful too.

'Without the struggle for food – that is, eating each other – they lose the urge to copulate,' I say.

'I hope you'll eat Larry, not me,' Serena says, 'and they put bromide in the soldiers' tea, and still they fought,' and I conclude, 'Maybe they fought for food, but now we don't eat our enemies, not even scoff the tidbits, though it's true we think of clever ways to kill, and make the meat inedible.'

We have arrived at a dead end, and we pause, a little gloomily.

She says, 'Now, hunting, shooting, importing animals and sharp dogs – that's one of the favours Larry gives. The others like it, he's quite indifferent.'

'Animals is quite another thing,' I say, 'we've got to think of humans,' and I remember some guy who says we've lost immediacy, see characters only on the screen, in paint, behind the stage lights all life is just a metaphor, or something we don't place at all, a threat maybe, or just outside our frame.

And then, the Chinese girl – for sure she's not outside my frame, but maybe I'm beyond hers – no history, no great identity, a brain alone just like that famous soft machine ... Serena has been talking, and I hear, 'The best thing is to leave – it's all this talking takes the edge off your resolve, it's all quite useless, compromise, as if you want to leave, nothing replaces that. You keep a little suitcase packed, and go! What more's to be talked about? And if they chase you, you can always call the cops – and they won't talk, the taser doesn't ask for compromise – revenge is never quite as good as absence – no one can talk you out of that.'

I ask myself, quite brutally, leaving the Engineer Harley far behind, 'Does Serena want Larry killed?' and aloud I say, 'It seems to me a nonsense', and perhaps I see her assess my powers as murderer.

It's like a game gone fierce. As if some kid's game, shooting nothing bullets into no-one, had turned, and real ones started pinging back, and Serena says, 'That's not a bad idea! One could maybe engineer that, only he doesn't game.'

'I for myself – if they caught me, I'd not like to spend the rest of my life working on a farm,' I reply but she's added a certain spice, if not a chilli sauce, to our fine sport.

'Maybe that Chinese girl could help us in some way,' she says, which seems to me absurd: she was ever a metaphor, the respected Chinese people snug in their stereotype are down to earth (look at the things they must have eaten) and the guardians of a mystery of which we occidentals will always be in awe and ignorant, a thing called History of which we've neither curiosity nor patience.

'True, she's a universe to be unlocked,' I tell Serena. It brings me back to the conference, the theme – to send a biscuit tin beyond the solar system, looking for beings preferably like us – and 'Why?' I ask, 'there's lots of people here we don't know stuff about, and plenty too who'd like to talk and we don't listen, not to mention things that's quite unlike we humans – lions, giraffes – no doubt with an agenda each, and we don't send a probe to them, so what do we expect, if they're like us, then star wars is the minimum, and if they're not, then what the hell, it's just for curiosity, maybe steal inventions if they've got them, or some grasses, go nicely in that vase, or animal in that cage – we've got enough, or just about, to last us through.'

'Larry is all brash, pretentious, but he's just the same as all his lookalikes,' I continue. 'To get away, you just should walk, and if you want to punish – well, there's no law against his wish to be immortal and command. It's what we all want, you for sure – only the Chinese girl's prepared to learn and listen for a while, then she'll be off and moving mountains, taking electricity from every stream—'

'That's done already, Harley,' Serena interrupts, 'and you're wrong to think she wants to be your pupil – something quite other there, I think.'

I make a picture in my mind, and maybe it's a dream I've sorted into actuality, a headline – something like 'Praga brennt', that smell of burning, familiar from before the first time, books and dogs and houses, all flamed up. I see a district, there's no green, no grass, a middle east of tin and yellow dust, the poor houses set well back, and richer houses maybe with a well you pay to use – and now it must be the old European war, a man, I think he has a tumour – but he is a resistance guy, he's trying to protect, or to seduce, a well-formed seventeen year old, and he has exported antique furniture for what – to support themselves or as a cover? Is he the good guy – here's another agent, come to order him 'return or be *infame*', treacherous – or will he stay, halfway seducer halfway traitor.

'Your father,' Seerna says, 'or was it perhaps your grandfather who's Czech, some ambiguity, but the message is quite clear – resistance turns into betrayal. I guess I should be warned, your family history's all there, no vision, Harley, just whatever you've made up to fit the facts,' and maybe it's all true, human, all too human, hard to throw that off, although with axioms you rub a lot of corners clean and plane away the knots and splinters too.

III

THE GUARD OUTSIDE my building waves his taser at the lion. The lion keeps his mouth shut so as to hide his feelings. I'm trying to avoid being a murderer, being an engineer seems less pertinent now, and there! I see the Chinese girl, waiting for me, what a surprise.

'I'm reading in your histories, your extrasolar project sounds like fun,' she says. 'And if you find some humans, way out there, according to the book you read, or say you do, discoveries will be massive. First thing, they should be speaking Hebrew. And who knows, instead of sin, maybe they played it cool, maybe it's still paradise, or yet again, by chapter two, when all the animals are ready, perhaps there was no flood and instead—' she looks solemn '—disasters of overbreeding, men overwhelmed by lions or just some creepy things, requiring intervention on a cataclysmic scale. The fuel project is another puzzle, suppose they missed the meteorites, the climate swings and all of that, but had no oil, no Middle East, no bombing of Baghdad, no caliph, even.'

'Oh no,' I say abruptly, 'you've not got that religious stuff! I really cannot answer all your speculations. All that I'm asked to do is something less than Larry's hopes of coronation in a world denatured, just sending a tin of biscuits, as it were, up above the clouds, and wash our hands of it, we'll all be dead before it falls back into some Russian bog and all our savings with it.'

She looks quite coy, and says, 'O come on now, Dr Harley, the two of us tied up in our space suits, plumbing the depths of emptiness', and she laughs, and maybe she's been laughing all this time, and now it all seems quite hilarious, to think of packing up my brain in some expensive tin and send it in the black to look for primal hominids – when really what concerns me is some quite banal and earthy sexual scheme Serena has in mind, for some obscure and useless punishment of Larry, guilty of being what he is and we're all glad enough to take his pay and laugh behind his back.

How banal it is, fleeing Serena, into the embrace of science. We – I and the Chinese girl – off in the simulator. Beyond the stars, beyond the solar system. I call her China, me she calls Harley. I say, 'We shall be dead before we're halfway there – if you can go to places without names, arriving in this pod, this tin ...' China says, 'It's all for science,' and she giggles, then, 'It's just a game, this stimulator – you must be brave', and I repeat, 'Before we get there we'll be dead for centuries,' if there's a 'there' to go to, dead.

China says, 'We won't go anywhere, it will just appear that way,' and they take us, wrapped like turkeys in our foil and special cloth that looks like shrouds, with tubes and such all sticking out, like we were in hospital, and I think, 'This way I'll never have to be a murderer – the price is my own suicide', and I start to wonder, is this Larry's scheme? Or is it maybe Serena's, a revenge – certainly she didn't want to let me go, a useful idiot indeed, and then they take us both, and put us in the 'helicopter' position, or so it seems, a special torture out of Africa, our hands bound to our feet, it simulates how we shall feel outside our system, but I know, from Eritrea to the US, they've all thought up some novel thing the body can't quite stand but not quite die – and wonder how we'll look to hominids all singing happily and eating fruit in that unsullied Eden way up there, they'll think we're mad to send two corpses in their last tormented state – maybe it's right, to show them what we have to do, to escape our lovers, or as China says, for science, and I add, for states and all that stuff and reading theory and the wrong books, or turning up our nose at massacre, and China says, 'We'll be all right if they shoot us out real fast, and I admire you, Harley, for this super trick.'

I'm quite unimpressed, she keeps on giggling and I say, 'I need some envelopes, some used ones, to write my calculations on,' and we can't see too much, just dials, some guys at consoles thinking of other things, and then I say, 'How long will this experience last?' and someone says – a tube deep in my ear, it pokes directly in my brain, a kind of tickle, terminal – 'The point is, we can't tell you, even near-death experiences are figured in, and absolute despond and desolation, crying in confined space and questions you can't answer, punishment without an end, without a trial, without a charge – it's all so useful, that you've volunteered, accolades and news surrounding you, though you won't know – the point is being isolated, with China here who values science, you as part of it perhaps,' and I wonder – who are the hominids we'll meet, the innocent, the pure ones? Maybe they'll see right into us, we sinners and our sins, I don't know if China's ever done something to regret, or if it's me – well, with Serena all has been quite innocent, or let's just say instinctive, or maybe you could say it's hedonism, so maybe it should be Serena here, sent off to meet her judges, though by that time she's dead, it's all quite biblical and silly, unless of course she knows that Larry has some crime he's done – deserves a punishment, at least in humanistic terms – and then, he should be here in this machine, trussed up by guys in those white overalls, and not Serena. And it's all banal, this talk of punishment and guilt and crime and torturing machines, and China's pleased and I am sure, despite her name she's never done a thing, maybe her country has or will by when we get there, wherever we're not going, but all she's done is follow me, my brain and mission, what a con and what an idiot she is, to ship with me eternally, a silly goose who can't protect herself, or even kick and bite ...

'He's not tranquil,' someone says, and here I am, these garage guys or gardeners or government employees of some low grade who're bending limbs as if we're those giraffes the magic guys make from balloons, but this is real – adventure without end, the purpose interpreted maybe long after we are just smears and slicks inside our super suits. Like turkeys.

I decide. I start to shout. They let us out. I hear them say, 'A brainy guy but no courage, no sense of adventure.'

China is angry. I say, 'That simulator can age us, send us to and beyond our deaths, more real than real, than looking out the window. The journey of a million miles, you remember ...'

She says, 'Don't call me China.'

'No offence – they used to call me Czech because my father, grandfather – others they called Chuck, same kind of thing,' and she repeats, 'Just don't call me China. What we missed would have been a real adventure.'

*

I think, I wish I didn't think it, that China is a person without substance. And now I'm back with Serena, Larry – no capsule, time slowed infinitely down. No hominids either.

Serena's amused by my simulator. 'It sounds quite you,' she says. 'What did your companion say?'

'That it wasn't torture, it was self-inflicted. And that if Larry is a bad man, time will sort him out, meanwhile ...'

Serena says, 'If we can't do away with him, he could always give me lots of cash.'

'But you don't want dollars, you want something else, a plan. Besides, that cash is magic, during the night it reproduces,' and for once she leaves the – our – divan, and I think that since I can't read character, don't know if she has one, good or bad, I could at least look at her decor – a print that says by Mondrian, but really from some show she's seen, the books, I flip them – *History of Color*, Simmel on Money, *Mona Lisa Overdrive*, *The Thief's Journal* – suggests a mind refined, inconclusive and confused. I put them back, a paragraph of each's enough to make a case, and then I think, 'Maybe they're Larry's, or a mix from both,' and she returns and says, 'But don't you think of running off – you at least I've got, to hold–'

I say, 'We're each free to take the walk, away,' and she just laughs, 'A little knowledge, Harley, gives us both a headache – we both know something more than cash was on our table,' and my other self, my Dr Engineer seems far away, it seems I'm just plain Harley now, accomplice, innocent and scared – just the worst things to be.

I say, 'I have my research', and in she jumps – 'It scares you, and you've got the Chinese girl in tow who wants to learn and steal, and you're afraid of where she goes – she pulls, and Larry pushes, poor Harley,' and I think, 'If you get in, you must be able to get out, not logical I know, many an ostrich in the killers' nets must think like that, it all ends bad, the pampas full of stolen children, necks cast down and severed, but still, they say there's hope, if not for you then some unknown, some brother, and don't be selfish if your life is shot and short,' but in my brain I'm up and running, plotting like a lion on bromide, because with her there is some link, without connections you're anomalous, however easier it seems to do without these fatal things.

Serena says, 'There's only three or four of us, things can be managed – not without wounds, I fear.' And I don't fear, I know.

*

Larry has disappeared. They say the simulator has been used. 'That doesn't mean a thing,' I say, but after all who knows? What can you simulate, back to philosophy, depending on what school you went to, or what church, we're standing on some rifts about what's real, I never had a doubt myself, but then with Larry, he's a trier, a real ambitious sceptic.

Serena shrieks, she says to me, 'You did it, did it for me.'

'Why would I?'

'We know Larry went much further towards slave trading than I said before, he split the cash with feistier friends who did the work,'

'You know I'm not the benefactor,' I say, to keep her quiet, 'not the justice man, don't even know what that might mean, still less to do it, just killing and then getting killed, it seems a stupid game,' but she's all over me ...

The Chinese girl is worried that they'll pick me up and taser me until I say I killed him, where'd I put the corpse, and why, maybe in the simulator, a virtual funeral, 'With flowers?' I say sarcastically, but she is scared and quite censorious – it seems that Larry is himself if not a saviour then a benefactor, better to have than not.

The cops come round, they put me in a van that smells of vomit, maybe the vomit's mine, and by the time I'm through, the whole system of the law – to me, all smells of vomit.

At the precinct there's a press of lions, quite used to being tasered, they throng around, eager for the tickle, and the cops oblige, a thousand volts or so will stretch your tail out, and to me the cops are friendly since they haven't got a corpse, and I repeat, 'Why would I?' and 'Maybe he simulated himself to something different,' and they laugh, they haven't got a clue, and all this stuff about the mathematics, which they call arithmetic, is alien ground.

The cops talk sagely of slavery, justice, jealousy, weapons. Larry, the missing object, what good was he, present or disappeared?

'Maybe someone threw him to the lions and they ate him,' I say.

The cops laugh. We all laugh.

'Surely you'd see a person in a rocket blasting off?' I say.

The head guy says, 'There's males all over, adult and not, that's blasting off, a kind of sexual ploy, always it ends bad – maybe your friend, your boss, maybe he planned a trip in space.'

'Really, space was foreign to him – everything for him had to be filled up. He'd never go where there weren't people like him, cutting him a deal,' but after all, if he's got a massive rocket somewhere concealed, he'd just shoot off to find a planet where they all play poker, organise in gangs, and yet have scientific knowledge that lets them play blackjack with packs of millions, have large-scale wars where no one dies, just dents a little ...

'Twinkle, Larry, Twinkle,' I think but do not say.

Perhaps Larry landed like a virus somewhere. But why'd he go?

'Yes,' says the cop. 'That's the question neither you nor I can answer,' and he puts it down to woman trouble, and he's likely right, how should I know?

The Chinese girl is worried, and she says, 'Come with me to China, there you're safe, or nearly so.'

I think 'never', but I say, 'There's all those people – and the food. And then the Wall – I don't think that's a good idea, quite inconclusive as it happens,' and she says, 'Of course, you love her – that Serena,' and she's wistful. 'Well, of course,' I say, 'just as you say so, on the other hand ...'

It's true that flight can be a proof of innocence, the getting out the way, not standing round as if you have some clue. Besides, there is my brain to feed, those plans I'm sceptical about. I need a place without those lions around my door, Serena's just another article on account.

I say, 'Well, maybe to Beijing I'll go. Go and be damned.'

IV

WE ARE IN OUR CAPSULE, really a good old aeroplane, high over somewhere. I'm disappearing too. Like Larry – or perhaps not like Larry. I'm going to China – with China beside me, which I mustn't say. Lots of ways to disappear – think of equations, think of stars, the last thing that you think of is a murder, by lovers or whoever.

Larry, rather his signature, will reappear, as long as banks transact – unless he's journeying to the stars, beyond our makeshift system, off to be – not lord of the universe, but maybe as consul in some tiny planet where they've never seen a despot, cast a ballot. The hominids dancing naked under those enormous trees, the animals not drugged but nuzzling up, gold crowns upon their heads.

I muse along, it seems the universal dream, though I may be the only one at this precise time in this tin pod to think these things. The girl says, 'You know that when we get there, I'm your boss?'

I say, 'I'm quite indifferent,' but that doesn't please, it's not what being bosses means to her, she sulks. I think about Serena, how she has another aspect, vulgar and vindictive she, I say aloud, 'It's all relatives,' and the girl beside me nods. You have to keep a distance, now it should be clear, I've no reason, no advantage, from a murder – and if he traded too in slaves, at this height, hard to tell who's slave, who's not, though sure as hell, nearer the ground you'd know. So – best to avoid the crime and punishment scene, the did and didn't, primal innocence or not – the girl sighs, says quite comfortably,

'I can't follow you at all, Serena must have had a terrible time,' and we float on.

I always preferred the puzzle, its beauty, to the solution. After all, each of us has partial solutions in their drawer. But there's only one puzzle.

The Chinese girl, now. Maybe the whole scheme was to coax me to Beijing, make biscuit tins stuffed with fortune cookies, lobbed through to Venus. 'Reply to sender, nothing hostile, please – you Venusians have a bad reputation in our books, though not, perhaps, in music. You have been warned.' And if the girl's some kind of spy, and aren't we all, electric telescopes are firmly in our wired-up eye – 'We'll seek it out, that spot of life that's hiding in the blue or black, a scaly worm up in some rock may hold the secret to our secret lives. We think, we joke. But be assured, no living frond, no mineral that creeps or burrows, no puff of air, up to one million degrees, will hide for long – for we have bigger plans, and bigger budgets than you guys on Venus.'

And so – forget the goings-on on various divans, the spaced-out lions, this disappearance of one crook or genius, patron of slaves. Remember Russian nobles with their orchestras of serfs, their master jewellers enslaved – our Easter eggs can now be starflung ...

And I sound a grouch, when really all I know is those few brainy things, maybe an instinctive thresh or two, need a divan, Serena too, but after all, in California or in China, things are much the same. Where one on one makes two, it's unmistakeable, and Larry minus Larry equals none.

It's clear that I know more about the scene than I will tell the cops – the same is true for them, they have a fantasy, and sources too, that fly beyond our system, a sketch of stories and of plots beyond the plausible, outside the observed.

But there! Enough! It's off to China, journey for a brain that doesn't move, that links up only things that can be linked.

Twinkle, Larry, Twinkle.

V

IT SEEMS TODAY it's got too hard to disappear. Serena writes to me – 'Harley, you sneak, betrayer, fugitive, you'll never understand how much I hated Larry. Your help alone I sought – although a touch more passion on your part would help to leave a sweeter scar behind. And now the bastard's gone, soul flying on some rocket, up to immortality. (Although I know you'll say it isn't really 'up'.) I loved you so, because I needed help, so I could cut the path I wanted. Yes, you did help, despite your fear of lions. And then you ran, you bastard too.'

Well, Larry's still a mystery. And as for lions, they must just stay in place, be there if ever they are needed – you propose and they dispose. So, where is Larry, gone beyond the stars, his project soaring though he'll be decades dead, whatever way he went? And still his slaves will track along the deserts and the seas. And there's the rocket, or its little biscuit tin, penetrating, black in the black. Nothing in nothing, searching maybe, or just lost and plotted.

And there is still the mystery of Serena. All that hatred. Lions at the door. The puzzles that you solve that don't solve anything – though even that can bring you cash and fame. And other, deeper mysteries too. Remembering the cemetery, high above the waves, for ever they repeat themselves. Rows of disordered marble tombs. And Kosovars who dance beside the sea.

FUNNY LITTLE FELLOWS

Foreword

IN THIS JOB, we learn to kill each other. In this job we learn to torture, no, not each other, that would be gruesome and grotesque, but whoever. To put it wholesomely, whomsoever. But we also get to see interesting places, people. People who don't kiss with their mouths – when you consider it, that's rather slimy – but with cheeks or noses, and who knows what comes after. But it's true, we live in violent times, a violent world, where we may all end up without water, without sun, even.

And yet, we must continue to discuss these things – write poetry, if you like, discuss how we know the world is real without us, whether we learn through things, or feelings, or because we're taught in a particular way – by who, I wonder – and of course many of the guys we deal with, that we try to educate in our civilisation – not that it always seems so great – anyway, they see the same things quite differently, and though they may drive Toyotas, even sniff some coca, or listen to our bands, nonetheless, their world is full of people to protect, situations to avoid like death, and enemies that are not ours. And may be us.

It takes no genius, in short, to see that though all things are one, and we are the one species – to stop the killing and the gouging and the stabbing, even the insults and the plotting, becomes a difficult and consuming business, where neither poems nor philosophy, nor even good intentions, help you much. Here a quite different set of ploys and escamotages comes into play, and we are talking different languages, although our actions seem identical to the other guys' – and even not too civil.

And so I find myself here, on the upward slope, a car is waiting, driver stubs again his oft-stubbed fag, we're almost off, the wires connect, and no one cheers but there's an air of celebration, a journey where we hope to learn.

Up Mount El'brus

THIS SWEET OLD Soviet car – at once stiff and bouncy – seems born of donkeys and pack horses. Up the mountain it goes, digging in with its buttocks, rolling with the corners. From up here maybe I shall see Mount Ararat, hovering above its ice like Fuji on the film packets – site of other nostalgias, other massacres. Remember the animals, clearly forced into the Ark – that beached on Ararat – as married couples, yet prevented in some way from procreation, God so angry, he hadn't realised that births would sink the ship, eat the crew. Then so penitent, but still with that problem of abundance. Chastity left to the animals. Abstinence however procured, a self-control to shame us all.

A mystery you can deal with at home, an adventure means you leave, immersed then in mystery. I've seen an ibex. I'm not what it is seeking. It licks a stone. At my feet ants are running like water. All life here is quite indifferent, as I should expect. Paths have crossed here. I have no path.

The tall old car keeps bottoming out. I yelp a little to Yuri Popov, and he laughs. 'You've got your own shock absorbers – you're sitting on them.'

We pass people waving. 'A glum life,' says Yuri.. 'Nothing to do and nowhere to go.'

To me, it's all a breath of the old world. I find a newspaper in the car, printed in one of the troubled provinces to the east. I expect Yuri will show them to me later as he takes me to the mountaintop.

The paper says: 'What'll we be eating in 2030, now

scepticism has taken over from the religious wave? Crocodiles, pigeons and sharks. What matter, as we all know it tastes like chicken. 'Streetwise pigeon legs on a bun. Croc paws sizzling.' The one thing that remains from the martyrs' death, now you can choose a 'splatter death'. After all, who wants to end up in a bed, a toxic pustule without kidneys, when you can go out like a man, gun blazing (with blanks maybe) against the Special Forces? The Terror is diffused, it's built in – like credulity. And the rich dissemble – the new puritanism leaves them protected from anything but local crime, yet still protesting ... And the end of nations doesn't end the universal anger. Anger, yes that's the mark of 2030. Our 2030 vision.'

I'm up here to find Oesho, god of the winds and high places – this mountain's measured as the highest in Europe, just a modest Asian one, a real confine, uncrossed by nomads but still full of corpses. Lord Curzon said the best frontier was a railway in the desert. No railway here. I turn my florid music up and make this terrifying view a symphony.

'For God's sake,' says Yuri, annoyed. 'This old style music everywhere – you should accept the modern turn – here, you can go to bed with anyone you like, or anyone you don't like. The edge is blurred between fact and fantasy, and anyway, what's wrong with fantasy, as the monkey said as he scored the winning goal in the world cup. Move on, old man, for "post" is always post and past, the merely modern is already dead, and we've the power to live the future we're inventing. We've learnt to say, "God save and fuck the planet and us with it, one step forward and one back, enough to see us through."'

Higher and higher. No bird, no tree. A cloud above –

and now below. No sound from those glum folks we passed. And Yuri says, ‘Battalions slid from here.’ I imagine them, the soldiers, they’re riding down the glacier, uniforms as for parade, sometimes a warrior fresh from literary duelling – the Pushkinites fought their battles here and fell right off the edge. Heroes of their time, then ever more dead heroes, poor dumb bastards.

We’ve reached the end of the track. We stand within a huge ice basin, basin full of ice that clinks like silver coins on shale, and sighs. Above is cloud, above and inside cloud – more mountain. Biggest in Europe. El’brus. There, it’s named, and so it’s not just rock, it’s real. As if some Spaniard tired of naming Indialand had sailed and beached up here. Maybe an Arab.

Below, far below, some soldiers are practising in a crevasse. Falling, raising each other up, and falling. A splodge of green that’s not of grass but uniforms. Voices disconnected, scared.

Yuri says, ‘It’s time to eat. The cooks got up at three to boil these eggs – a minute more and they’d be edible.’ They’re soft and mucous. He hurls his into the glacier, and I think poor unacknowledged chicken, and throw mine after. A century, and they’ll slide down with the soldiers, those faces red as apples, dead, the eggs now grey, grey green.

I say, ‘I guess we’re hardboiled eggs’, but Yuri is fixed on death, and now eternity, ‘Where there’s no time and no events, eternity is infinitely long and also infinitely short. In fact it isn’t anything. So don’t expect to meet your granny or your pets. No hope to keep your eye on things – without duration there’s not any thing. And so, your robbing banks, your judgement, penitence, it’s all over and never begun, no trace left on the ether.

Which there isn't anyway.'

We look gloomily up to Moscow, over to Berlin, then there is Georgia and down there Teheran, and Yuri says, 'These high mountains – there never is a top, a needle point to stand on – just another saucer full of ice. Here, at least, we have the glacier, creaks and chinks with grey and silver planchets, then, as if it has a motor, movement, seeming to promise life – but really – just slides inertly.

'Fields of force, spirits in trees. You see, the people here,' he points south and east, 'and the people there,' it's north and west, 'are just pools, of people, like they were animals in a forest. Only when they're brought together, like herds, like hordes, – you bring them all together, the hot and cold, believers and not, the animists and the people of the book and word who hate each other, like people together on an ark for maybe a millennium – get pissed off, prefer to drown or throw the others overboard, so much for diversity and stuff like that. Taken one by one, these humans are quite lovely, you'd want to make a set, collect the cleanest ones, but – tough – what you get's exactly what you haven't seen. A surprise packet, some want to screw you, others prefer the longer squeeze, to milk you for a lifetime then, in the name of friendship, set you free. Your last years. Anxiety, waiting for the doctor's nod.'

He asks me, 'Who you spying for?'

'And you?'

'Who do you think?'

He's got on a pair of dirty trainers and smudgy pants, but a beautiful black jacket – must be made of shaven ape-skin or some such, and his face hair's sculpted round, two scimitars of dark sideburns reaching to the jowl, a line of tough moustache, like Seventies cinema Mexes. A thoroughly modern anomaly, excellently prepared for show and yet it says 'keep off', and if you get too close, 'fuck off, I'll hurt you'.

He says, 'I understand the spying urge. The curiosity. But spying is for, about, something, or, rather, it's for someone.'

I say, 'We're all a little spooks, all trained to be a spook, it doesn't matter if you do it for the truth or to plan a heist or tell a government who to kill.'

He isn't satisfied. He says, 'If you could see anything from here' – a mist's come down, below, the soldiers practising their falls, down in the crevasse and out again, are deep in trouble – 'if you could, you'd see right down into Georgia, where they say America begins. And over to the left there's sea, two Romes, and to the right the troubled lands and then downhill to China and the porcelain, the tea, and take another wiggle and you're with the magic monkeys, shapeshifters and the valiant deeds of battling lovers, seeking some grail or just a quiet screw ...'

I say, 'In Georgia, they make you drink a bottle of brandy every time you sit at table – how can you function there?'

'You don't have to drink it,' he says, 'and besides, they are our long-lost, never-found – our brothers by a different father and perhaps a mother too, maybe just all huggermugger in the barn, it really doesn't matter, who could care after all these years?'

I say, 'Maybe to you it doesn't matter—'

'Then who does it matter to, and so – it's true that you can buy friends, but they never will be loyal slaves, they'll always be available for sex but it's all a little slow and boring, and for anything else it's just more money, just more cash, though fortunately it all comes back as commissions – and to pay the services of you and me.'

All these little countries, clans cobbled together, myths reinvented, cultures with diasporas immense, faiths swelling and deflating. Steadfast or forever mutated.

I say, 'And these little criminal entrepots, a myriad of hotspots all competing,'

'Just civic pride,' he says, 'like football fans. Allsorts in a bag.'

And now the soldiers are upon us.

*

Reality is a crevasse on Mount El'brus. I'm dangling like a paralysed spider – below, a misty cold cauldron of nothing but air, the soldiers say, 'We need a counter-weight,' and I think 'not me' and they're on me, wrapping me all round, just enough pressure on the throat and ribs to make me squawk and see it all, near-death, the sea, the dead fish, wallflowers, the dark well, and then I'm dangling down, in the crevasse. Above, the silly grinning heads of soldiers. Gone are any tales of gals and heroes, faith in reason, now it's all just dangle. I shout, 'Who will be my counterweight?' Some faces disappear, I see a larger gap of sky, no light. And there is soldier Anatol, white as a curd and up and past me, and I go down, where ice is green and smells of nothing, filling up my lungs, and down I lurch again and laughter or maybe it's curses like I'm the dreg in a green bottle and then they pause ... 'Who you're spying for,' maybe I hear, 'The Muslims, Georgians, tribes?' No one, and so no protection, we explorers are all a bit of spook – 'liberal, communist, atheist', and I hear them say, 'Suppose we use some of this old military junk and hoist him up,' and I suspect that Popov's taken over, one spy can't lose another spy, that changes all the rules.

What looks like sticks but must be guns comes slowly down, and I go up, revolving. Popov is laughing as I reach the top, still spinning.

Then down we go, in the car, white into green, the people peering from their huts; old Ladas now are chicken mansions, the children stare and pick their nose, we're back in the human melting pot that never melts, that keeps the clans alive and feisty, and here a church and there a blackened little mosque and vice versa and so on and on through borders and some checkpoints and at times Popov is scared and undesirable, and sometimes it is me, though my fine shoes work better than a visa – better than his jacket – it shows that I've the might of wealthy men, somewhere at my back, who can command. And here I'm in this bar, there's several clans all spitting at each other, across the tables, but it seems it's some kind of detox place, maybe for hangovers as there isn't any drink, just a tall fire, and someone says 'More rose petals', something is thrown, the flames leap and the smoke gets in our throats and legs. And there's this ice-white woman, Petra, and she sits with me, and maybe I'm in love and surely never will forget, and at a point she bites, she bites. It's like a viral snake, she bites me deeply in the cheek and there is blood and laughter, more rose petals, and she says, 'You want kids? I can have all you want and more besides,' and she's all over me, and there's my passport done the rounds, and though it's false it seems Canadian – with one of those no-one's to know where you have been and what you're after – and she's my spirit and my sickness and I know this wound is epic and will leave a scar right through. And someone says, right in my ear, 'His favourite pig followed him right to the slaughterhouse.'

And – peace, yes, peace. Like the icy basin where the glacier starts, the bodies under glass, just starting on their slide, the soft-boiled eggs an offering to no one in particular. And not a bird, the mountain's dome dissolves in mist, and mist below, the soldiers all gone home, the live ones, and the dead just slowly trucking down. And yes, it's peace, but not eternal.

Popov has saved my life, I think. I say, 'Call me Stag.'

'Not your name.'

'Not my name.'

All those guys, those kingdoms, wave a paw to Georgia, Ossetia, the Caspian, Khwarezm – where the cultured pillagers came from – their different gods, the languages from who knows where, Georgia full up with Armenians, homelands of Iranians and Turks, the Russian clans, a restless wandering from field and steppe and forest, seeking a better creed, more better creeds and yet when all is said, just looking for a crust, a piece of cheese, a bottle without the hangover.

'And all too human, my young spy!'

I have a debrief with my chief. Skullface by name and looks. He likes to make it seem it's our first time.

'Name?' he asks.

'Stagg Delfine.'

Skullface asks about the Stagg.

'Some guy lent money to my father. Mortgage on my name.'

He says, 'Well, when you work here, lots of things are

provisional. Some you can pay off.' He points to my cheek. 'Fine set of tooth scars there.'

'Thanks.'

Assigned to tea. Teapots. Tibetan tea, Indian, Chinese, Sogdian, Turkic even, in bricks, alembics, poems, terracotta friezes, ritual, grave goods, on camels Bactrian or not, on birchbark and on silk. He asks, 'The trade itself? The routes, prices, flows and politics, and who's behind. As cover you must write a book – a serious book, remember.'

I say, and it's not all wrong, 'The publishers want a picture book.' He wanders off quite satisfied. I can't read all the sources anyway, can't reconstruct the whole mosaic.

Tucked into this observatory, institute, researching everything – the keyholes, bombs, imperatives of faith, the trousers up or down, outrunning any man's predictions – a network of obscure things, pressures on this guy here, that produces bankrupts over there, some law no law unto ourselves, a massive card game with anonymous players – all connected up with intelligent glue. No director, no researcher, ever letting go or closing – each obscure thing tied to the next, proclaiming history and the unexpected, causes, effects, unreasoning logic. One luminescent string knotting to the next ... length of string.

I like the rituals, but the taste of tea comes to disgust. Maybe in my memory there's that tea in Paraguay, that maté and the coca, tasting and sniffing, taking up the gun, sucking the silver straw, the memory that spurs the blood. Inventing what we'd like to forget, and perhaps is only story, the monkey says 'feeling guilty about your past crimes takes the pleasure from the new ones'.

Lady gurus here, beautiful, but just to make the tea.

And Skullface muses, 'Popov may be hired. If he wants. I must send him some good shoes.'

I ask, 'What can he offer?'

'Well, he says he saved your life, and knows the embroidery of the clans that make us up.'

'Well, he cast me down,' I say grudgingly, 'down in the ice cave, then he said to pull me up – if that is saving life, then he's the greatest.'

'It's him, or there's a lady major that they want to send, and maybe she's from China, or it may be,' he pauses, 'she's just Chinese, so could be from anywhere at all, believing who knows what or absolutely nothing.'

And I think of Anna, who might be my friend, my lover. She's already here. She says of Skullface, 'He's quite funny sometimes,' and it's her I feel for, but she says, 'I'm still in love with George.'

'George the Georgian? That's a safe bet, since he's dead. He's your protection now – a real longing for an unreal object. Beyond the stars.'

I say, 'If China lay beyond that door, I'd go.'

But will she come, the major? Popov had saved my life, he says, and so he's coming, now he's here, and life goes on. And Petra bit me, and has left her mark. Left, too, a little grave figurine, back from the steppe, earth mother, maybe, or Cybele, borrowed from someone else's myths.

The major writes, and jokes, 'I'm waiting for my horse', the aeroplane is like a horse and so I say, 'A horse would go down well here. Carrying the tea, at least partway,' it seems she knows us all, the institute with its ghostly crew, and maybe by divine right she's mine, since Anna still belongs to George.

And Anna says, 'I'm your best friend, and but for your nerves, we'd be together still.' 'My nerves! You got on them, that's why,' I say.

Her face is quite Byzantine, each feature taken separately is soft, they melt together and you have a calm tough ensemble, low arches, caramel depths, silks and pink that could be set in stone or any hard metal. She says, 'I'm a bitch, you know,' and then, 'You're wrong, perversely wrong.'

I ask, 'Old Skullface, how d'you find him?' And she says, 'We're lovers sometimes,' and I'm appalled. 'Why him?'

'Well, he's the boss, of course.'

And 'When?' I ask.

'Mostly in motels. At lunchtime.'

'What, pillows and sheets, all that?'

'Sometimes he's quite funny,' she repeats, and goes on, as if it doesn't matter, copulating with the chief, 'Who are all these guys you're dealing with? Regime judges, torturers, slave traders, grannies sold for cash ... Who are they, your chums? If ever I'm to help you, I need to touch them, smell them, look into their eyeballs, cost their dental work, the tic, twitch, beating vein of complicity.'

But I'm obsessed, I say, 'No, not with Skullface. Not bed. Not absorption, pleasure if you like, or social climbing, or to satisfy, but repetition, no!'

'Of course.'

'Bed? Pillows and sheets? Blankets even?'

'Motels at lunchtime,' and I think, you could have brought sandwiches, eaten them at your desks.

What sense of humour rustled between the sheets? My warmth was all bled out, high on the glacier, high above the clans that fought, each with a language untranslatable, inherited, a mouthful of melon seeds, parched thistles, spit and spit.

And later Skullface says, 'We're here to stop the universal crumble – even fat old Mr Capital, too fat he can't roll over in his bed, we're here to do what he can't do, confront the little bands of sad and evil people in the mountain tops, the cities, if live in them they must – just tough on them.'

I say, 'Everything always crumbles.'

'Yes, but we have at least the choice. First we defeat our enemies, then we can choose – a willed extinction. The big chiefs say – enough of holding on, waiting for history to take another turn – world regret, the Germans had a word for it. Enough of this fading foliage, bodies all rusted out, enough of transplants, therapies. Why let the flawed endure?' He pauses, rests a knee on my desk, he is very tall, and I see his suit is stained with ink, with liquid ink like they used to use. And then he spoils his vision: 'Now, dear Stag, just follow me in my little wandering – the aliens. Remember, they always followed our technology – saucers that flew when we still had five o'clock tea. Then discs – our backs were bad, and later still the implants, body takeovers, when the whole bony part begins to wilt. And now, just think of viruses – not just the ones the chickens have, but laptops. In our computers, yes, there's lots of sickness that we humans plant, but there are too,' he pauses. 'Funny little fellows. Not just destructive, but masterful. Sussing our secrets. Changing the names, speaking with tongues. Getting even to our monkeys, biblical, Koranic – all the wise masters, some of them with beards to scratch. Funny little fellows. Aliens – viruses – in our laptops.'

*

Our Institute. Beneath are miles of galleries – first the monkeys, smelly but sociable among themselves, then the departments of bilocation and shapeshifting, the narcotics (locked), smoke sneaking through the keyhole.

I say, 'Tea is not a strategic good.'

'Maybe not at first, but widely used, a driver of the bureaucratic effort. Besides, once we found the monkeys reproduced the bible and could write an infinity of others, everything became a precious option. The world became strategic, its past and present, everything at all, auguries for the future, if there is one. Every little thing a passe-partout, only connect – now everything's connected, one big system, all is filed and latent, and the dead—'

'The dead?'

'Nothing to be done with them, except they're there. Alongside. An earthly paradise, like dinosaurs that end up in the shale, as oil, that drive your old Camaro. Dino juice that's squirting out the back and up your nose.'

I say, 'But then again, there's the intentions. The spying game's not just into what is, research, intelligence, but where you plant your bomb, spike the drinks, insult the women...'

'Well,' says Skullface, 'I've shared some secrets and some remedies. So now I'll tell you how you fit. You see, to set up things like peace and maybe war – though war's an altogether easier track – we need a fresh, a charismatic face. In short, we need a celebrity. We, of course, look after the charisma bit. Not to make gravitas, you understand, but a real, a wholesome icon. Someone to stick on the wall, to put it rudely. Someone for dinnertime. The screen is throbbing – suddenly it's you!'

'But people don't want stirring, wishes fulfilled. They want today.'

'Some space remains. Day on day, some dreams they have. The people twist and turn, they calculate, they go out in the streets, they scream, they battle, stab and chirp. They're what we always were, and what they are is what we have to fix.'

'It seems old hat.'

'And *vieux chapeau* is what you are, my friend. And that is what we need.'

So each big cheese has clinging to them one little cheese – or more.

He talks about the institute. 'Just type in WORD OF GOD and you'll see how clever the monkeys are in writing software – the whole text, complete with all the begats – a real puzzle for the monkeys at first, who don't set store by ancestors.

'I told you how the bosses have decided – plan for the end, quiet Armageddon. Leave it to the aliens, if they want – they're already here, and so you end the mess, the torture and the slaughter!' He laughs, goes on, 'We're in a criminal war zone. The favourite pig trots affectionately to the slaughterhouse, the old school friend's shot on someone's orders, alighting from the train on the way to his new job. And those little pools of evil-doing – Naples, Mexico City, the cities and the regions that live by contraband, enslavement of the best – the better thing is: turn them into micro-states. That live by contraband and enslavement of the best. But then, they'll have an army and police, ambassadors and all that stuff, and so you set the good bads against the bad bads. Our national states are hopeless, no, you need the war of each against all and in the end they'll all turn out like us, but much too small to do the kind of damage that we've done, we do. These nasty little city states, these bands of brothers, in the end will fuse quite easily with the larger world of capital. Money, they say, has neither colour nor a smell, and so they'll tip their cash back in the pool.'

I insist, 'Who are these mega-archs, how do they decide we're for extinction. And all the election stuff ...?'

He laughs, 'You don't suppose they let those little guys and gals, those ephemera, rule the roost? They put them up, they cast them down. No one is the wiser. Indeed, wisdom doesn't enter.' I persist. 'How are the top guys chosen, who chooses them?'

'If you know that, if I were to tell, then you'd know everything.' And I suspect he doesn't know. He leans over me. 'You know, Anna is our link with crime,' and he adds, 'You know, you may have heard, my predecessor had a most mysterious wife – in her youth she'd been an acrobat, and worked the best circuses in Europe. She was called the most dangerous woman in the continent.'

'No, it can't be so,' I say, 'I used to know them both, she kept out of sight. A true homebody, wouldn't even keep a dog.'

But he is heavy with his news, and says, 'As far as I'm involved, the Chinese major can be yours, if she shows up. She and your saviour, Mr Popov, both have lived it all, if not in first person, then in history. Here in the Institute, we don't confuse the ordinary mechanisms of social control, irksome those these are, with visionary repression. Not that we propose, nor oppose, repression, just cast a cold eye. And if you want to change the habits, what they call the culture ...' and he lays a burning eye on me, and I remember Anna saying, 'He's quite ardent.'

'For you,' he says, 'the plan is this – a charismatic celebrity, concocted, to make a day of peace for the whole world. A day without a death. Maybe to give a taste.'

I say at once, though he's not asked me, 'I think it's stupid. On Monday we don't fight, refresh our wounds and clean our guns, and next day we are at it, fighting for diamonds or justice, as relief.

Better to plan how to live in it, the zoo is better than the jungle – war's in our nature, however much we dream of second chances.'

'Yes,' he says, 'so, it's quite stupid. But that's quite harmless, if we pull it off. Inflating you, and riding with the rhetoric.'

'Why, then? Just for the risk the system needs? Conflict's a thing we clansmen do, it suits us, gives us identity. Modesty should be the mode.'

'No clan would take you, Stag,' he says. 'Besides, up on the mountain, it wasn't cash that drove you.'

'No, I already had the money.'

'Pay.'

'No, curiosity. The money won on horses.'

'A prize? Scholarship?'

'No, a horse. And curiosity. And I got bitten. Though not by a horse.'

He is not dismayed. 'Well, anyway, why else d'you think we'd want you here?'

I say, 'There in the basement, past narcotics, there's the eventuality room. There, I believe, they calculate all possible outcomes, occurrences, disasters, alliances – the switchback of the nations, rise, fall, rebirth – and above the clouds of angels, rising, falling, they estimate what this angel, devil, criminal, accomplishes. And best thing is, I hear they sell these possibilities as scripts for TV and the movies – even a division that cloaks it all as sex or epics. I think that there's my home and destiny.'

'But no,' he laughs, 'that's just where we make our money, thinking of futures – that's our nature too. The zebra never thinks his world could be unstriped. And yet, we plan, take the stripes off. And planning's what we've done for you.'

*

A flaw in the computer, and I've new unwanted friends. Clicked into pervasive life.

A Dr Afasian, maybe survivor from my mountain farce, Armenian by name and habitation – who can tell? – from Moscow, Tbilisi, all references mushed together, Armenians like oil in machines long rusted out, even in Egypt, taking on the burdens of others less articulate, adding to all the burdens already taken on ... Proposing a politics parallel to the task they've given me, but with discoveries, even deviant.

And a Mr B, a Mr Beest, I think from somewhere in the Americas, usual computer come on, make some money give me your identity, history, who the hell you are, Jew or Arab, maybe a Japanese all with their baggage that they have to have, info equivalent to precisely nothing much, tales for the kids and maybe somewhere there's a walking skeleton, a granddad survived who makes the story all his own, but now the thing is just to make back the cash the previous trickster lost for you, first thing's to believe with all your heart, yes in yourself, but also that big frosty mountain, Capital, just waiting like a frozen turkey for your knife.

And Cai, is she Chinese, maybe from Vietnam, or then again it could be jokers from Mumbai or Bangalore who know this script and so can shapeshift into any mode and any story that they please. She promises adventures to the past, an ABC – an ancient book. Tract of philosophy, one of the books a Chinese emperor ordered burnt, its author, along with 13,000 others, executed, and yet the book survived, up there in the rafters.

Maybe Mr B's an alien, a virus, thing with no beginning and no fate, and yet from somewhere, and Cai is telling me about her struggle to acquire some plumbing and has ended up, she says, with all the glory of a toilet without water – the pipes required all lying in some pile, a scam by warlords or a bureaucrat – and what has this to do with philosophy I ask, and it's too late, she's off in Ming or maybe Tang philosophy and metaphor, the poems sound to me like Japanese and improvised. And then she says, 'You're crazy, putting a system of values in your politics and economics, bound to end in tears, hypocrisies all round. Better to see it all, freefalls and eye patches together, our common, equal humanity, all in one boat, some captains and some slaves, all in the end condemned to eat each other.'

Afasian says, 'If you want change, you must act quick, and really want it, otherwise the economy recovers and they're all back and digging in the fields and shopping, and so – on and on the great ship sails, the captain being drunk or overboard – it really doesn't matter since what makes it go is wind. Is wind, my friend.' He sounds infinitely sad, sad as the infinite stupid wind.

And Mr Beest says, 'If it's celebrity you're bound to be, there must exist a process of development. Not just a string of ceremonies and secret lives, you must aspire, from ingenuous victim and spy to win some kind of command.'

Cai says, 'This sage, this writer, had in mind that aspects of the musical art were dangerous. For that he suffered, and he hid. Or rather, he concealed.'

'Music? Intervals, melodies, words maybe.'

'No, really it was mathematics.'

'Numbers – it's all intervals, up and down or horizontal.'

'Not really. More it was mechanics. A building programme that the emperor had wanted would be blocked by inauspicious calculations.'

I say, 'But surely, then, the advice was good, a little wiggle would have unblocked the destiny.'

She pauses. 'Not really. The idea was to block the nomads by building them a city. Nomads supplied the horses needed, so a city meant that price and supply were fixed – so too the nomads stuck behind the city walls. Nomads can't defend a city, and when they do, they're settled, part of the pack. A city's good for artists and the like, for show, parades, the beautiful people walking up and down. The tourists.'

'So this guy's advice was a political refusal, advice for the nomads to stay as they were.'

'So it would seem, did seem.'

I'm curious and I ask, 'What are you, Cai, an avatar like my Afasian and Beest, or real, with sex and wages, insurance – all that stuff?'

There is a pause, maybe offence. She – for let me fancy it is she – replies, 'My hair is darkish, I'm about one metre seventy. Majored in human studies – I like music, reading, keeping fit.'

I think of Anna, and the giggling in motels. I wonder

if they used the same one, or had a rota on the Strip.

And later Cai, mine by divine or Skullface's right, says, 'I'm not real Chinese, just one of their minorities,' and I want to ask if from the steppe or wetlands, mountains or deserts, but she asks, 'If they want to give you fame, can't you use it to say something a bit significant, or even biting,' and I tell her, 'All the celebrities try that.'

Afasian talks of structures, though Beest says that's all revelations and no good, just need daily grind – but Skullface seems to have a link with Cai, and I'm surprised that Cai the writer, now my colleague, should be one, the writer not just fiction, Cai the major moderately feisty. And Mr Beest tells me of a Hindu and a Muslim arguing over who should date a highly polished Indian lady, going to insults, 'Pigeater', 'Monotheist' though both are vegetarians and atheists, the lady has a fine grey cat, a tail held upright like a feather, and she no doubt discreet with other lovers and so haughty ... And I wonder if that lover is Mr, maybe Doctor, Beest, and he goes on, capitalism, war, the rules you must obey, and science being full of rules, all marching along in lockstep, and we just poor anarchic warriors who never fight because our market value lies in being without wounds, there just as a threat.

'After the trivia,' he says, 'comes the dominating abstract, after the bathos, heaving movements – the transportation of the "tea" – though no one drinks it here' and I wonder where 'here' is, 'the horse trade, art, the guns, banknotes, and above it all, the cloud above the glacier, the mountain top, if it has a top but must have, logically ... Above them all: Monsieur le Capital.'

I tell him, 'It's all in order', and I turn away and ask, 'Are you the Cai who writes? The same one that's arriving?' And she repeats, 'in order here', but I'm not sure, the ghosts that use computers now have quite confused who's real and who's on payroll – but Cai is here, she takes me on a ride. As we proceed – a kind of festive shed, long tables clad in copper, and there's men, men in sheepskins, metal boots, that's dancing up a storm. And somewhere there's a band or maybe it's a tape that's going wild and screaming high with violins and trumpets and some maniac who's drumming so's to lose the rest, and they are deeply in their brains and won't wake up to anything except their whirling on, and I think 'Sufis', but it's more Tex-Mex, or maybe Bulgars, with a touch of drugs and maybe raki or a slug or two of something made from apricots, that maybe leaves you blind but just the moment when you took it down, you see the future and the past in one unyielding moment – eternal time that is no time at all. And thank you, God, for you were right, a billion years last just one slice of second, and we know all that you know, though true – we can't create a sound or tree or chicken, any goddam thing, and one god is perhaps better than all the panoply the guys are invoking here, the drumming on the tables, on the tapes ... And now the guys that's dancing like they've redhot boots are joined by little imps with packets of black powder, like powerful squibs – they throw the bags, and splaffs beneath the feet, the air is full of flash and flup and whap. And on they go, nothing will call a stop, unless it's something arbitrary, and I think, 'they must be copper miners' but there's too much goddam noise to hear my thoughts. And then Cai takes me to a cave, or maybe it's a tomb, or church, or arsenal and we must prostrate ourselves and hell, it's some religious theatre with a play, it seems to last for days, but no, it lasts for weeks. And all the pain at last dries up, because we're numbed by lying there, and I can hear the guys still dancing on the tables in the other zone, and priests galore and smells and pills for everyone, our brains have all leaked out like custard and have joined the one big superbrain or mushroom soup that's forming in the roof, and I can't feel, not pain nor love nor anything, my comrades or my enemies just palpitating here, no start, no finish, no subjection, just a little taste of being quite alert, and yet not being anything at all.

When that is done, we all stand up, though who we all are, I've no idea, and then I see we're in another mode, and here is fire, a fire altar and some threatening guys, and various gods rise from the smoke, and then there's movement.

'But these are state religions, all controlled.'

'Wait and you will see where all that comes from,' says Cai.

'One thing or the other, they're either spontaneous or the state,' I say.

She is angry. 'It isn't that at all,' she says, 'there is no chaos, there is no disorder – it's either present or it's forming', and I think, 'At least it's not all done with animals,' and I hear my voice aloud, 'No, not the animals, at least leave the animals be', but it's the start of sacrifices, and I wish they'd get on to the humans who at least believe they're doing it for good, if not exactly fun, although I guess they've had a good time before death, at least the night before, the little kids seem to get off on the idea of pretty clothes and paradise before the knife ... And now the animals have gone, they've gone into the fire, and now it's humans, maybe prisoners or maybe not, the chosen ones, unfortunate for sure and knowing it or not, though after all a good priest can put you down without a squeak, it's just like surgery, and so you do not wake, there is no pain, and nothing ...

And so, having atoned for what I know not, now we all swarm out. Then we have a little entr'acte given by the maidens – if they are such, and you've got to go a long way to find some simpering tuneful virgins in these parts – wherever these parts may be. But there's an air of kindness, discovery maybe, a quieter time. Thank God the drummer's had enough, and so have we, we lie here on the earth, the sky is very low. At least each has his own brain again – but no, off we go once more, and now it's war and maybe social justice, we're in two teams, we snarl and scream, we've all got sticks or maybe clubs – nothing that let's you finish off your mate with just a single blow, so doing it's quite serious, smash and smash. Adrenalin, if it is that, helping to support the gravest wounds, you lose a leg or finger and you go on as if you've batteries inside.

So, is this chaos, or an order rigid, predetermined? And maybe we'll go ahead for days or years, not doing much and planting maize and then perhaps to build a city, start some trade or carve a rock and paint our faces.

Now I understand why Skullface says celebrity is something that can take us out of this: real sentiments for unreal objects, not the king, but the meta-king, not the guy that tortures you but some nonentity who keeps you interested and if you're lucky even a laugh or gesture of disdain. But keeps you in the loop.

*

From somewhere between Turfan and Lanzhou, Cai once had her home. Unlikely she was on the caravans, few nomads make it to the secret police, the Cold Mountains still all sorts of barrier ... Her history spread out like a map – one or two roads, some details to be pencilled in, though spellings change, moustachioed adventurers had changed their language and technology. And I remember the tattooed Mongolian in Moscow, sitting at my table and laughing as no food arrived, the dishes on the menu last seen in 1916, his life a line of mirth. My history has no map, it's just a vapour trail, nothing abandoned, all just moving on.

*

I intercept a message, Skullface to Cai. He says, 'Stag's a fine lad, an empty vessel. Has infantile concern with, fascination for, violence not as a by-blow but a thing in itself, not tactic but a strategy of the species. And though he may be right, yet he will do, and with this preoccupation will do perfectly. And tea will bind us all! – as has concentrated England in these last two hundred years, and spreads, and now dear Cai, with comrade Popov, if you can tolerate him, you'll bind us to Stag's project. Those land routes turning into concerns quite abstract, we call them geopolitical – but still a vital flux.'

'But he must have positions,' she says, 'not just aversions?'

'He's no beliefs – I won't say has no qualities. Doesn't know where he stands, not having faiths, religion, ethnic roots – whatever you may think these are. He's a tower of winds, he stands there and is ventilated by whatever breeze – and only fears a tempest when that means demolition. He's curious because he's ignorant. We took him, knowing nothing about anything. To him, life's just aesthetic – it pleases him, or not.'

*

Afasian writes, 'My friend, you must see I'm an extremist, my great temptation – tear it all down and build it up another way. Decoupling, that is still the word. Take Islam, ride it for a while until it's clear it's only faith – which I have none – but after it has mobilised and shaken thrones! And capitalism – dies and ends and is reborn, the dragon coming from its cave, but ... Whoa! not father dragon, but the son or daughter, the fire is just the same. And once again, off with its head, but meanwhile from the cave – and call it capitalism or what you will – it's just our sneaky nature coming forth, to eat our brother – giving him a hand, screwing our sisters, all in the family, and on and on. But what I'll suggest to you, my friend ...' But I close him off, banal stuff, prelude to some scam that means just signing things, there being little else to do in ether – except to snuggle into someone else's bank account.

And Mr Beest, or surely it is Doctor or Professor Beest, he too has some scams to offer, not the apocalyptic political kind, which lead you just to tears or worse, not international bonds, but innovation.

'Listen, Stag – there's nothing now for you to make from finance – what you need is something everyone will want. And sell and sell till everyone has got one, like it was another thumb or leg, and based on our humanity. Need a phone call to your granny, watch the tickertape, latest massacre or famine, maybe a flood or cops on heat or any goddam thing? But this is genuine.' He pauses for days. I wonder if he's selling to hundreds like me. 'The new deal's personalising. Everything – identity. Who you are like, identical to, your twin, your enemy, your avatar. Making it more real for you, beef up your piddling imagination and scarce facts – everything you have that makes a picture, no larger than the inside of your head.'

He raves on. 'I propose that everyone should carry a sort of autobiographic sheet, all electronic, naturally, that the person next to them can read. They just plug in. It's a version of your life, who you are, would like to be, your skills and interests. It's what I call the Personal Card. The great thing being that every day, in every way, you edit all the details. Today your Spanish granddad takes the fore, tomorrow it's archery your forte, then it's some epic or a personal creed – maybe Gilgamesh becomes your favourite book. And no one criticises, says you're an arrogant or a selfish person because we know: tomorrow it can, will, and should all change, and disappear and in new forms – it reappears. Yesterday you were, today you have become – tomorrow, more epiphanies. That way we make our own histories, and so new history is made, but very brief and shifting. And all of us will have the Card. No need to speak. You're who you are today, newly invented, silent and untouchable.'

He goes on: 'I'm standing in the bus and just plug in to A or B beside me, and I have their story. Maybe they want to be an acrobat, a suicide, or sleep with nuns – you never need to say a word, or tell them that you're reading them, or questioning if it's all made up or deeply felt. You see, we share in each other's fantasy,' and I think of the wife of Skullface's predecessor – certainly a vulgar confusion of names and persons. He goes on, 'Because, young Stag, feeling deep has nothing at all to do with what you really are, because what you put on your Personal Card is real and what you really are, and feel.' He is triumphant. 'Think of the cash we'll get! The whole world needs one – not some state document, your height, religion, all that crap, that mostly you can't change – although I have a scheme for changing height that's only at the start – but something that is you, and made and modified by you, unknown to all authorities ...'

'But the police?' I say. 'Thought crime is here again, and if you put down on your card you stole a fish, for sure they'll charge you, make you stand a trial, although it didn't happen.'

'You have a point. It isn't proof against the torturer, who'll make you tell the real from real. But that is easily overcome. If you find the going's tough, you cancel instantly, without a trace. Deny it all. No one will ever know.'

I insist. 'But that way you are blank sheets, they can make you confess to anything, and so you miss the option of keeping to a prudent silence – or a modest lie.'

'That's true, but what's your point? If everyone stays silent and anonymous, we are all everything – you're quite secure, and quite irrelevant. The only thing you mustn't do – is get caught in the act, the act of cancelling yourself. And after all, so many of us never accomplish anything. The Card, well, yes! It's an accomplishment, and if you're caught, unlikely, – but then, c'est la vie, me boyo!'

There's more recruiting, interviews, we nominate acquaintances we think won't threaten us. I'd known Harry before. He had handed me to Yuri Popov, as he put it, for protection. Now Skullface wanted to appoint him – internal security.

Skullface says, 'Describe him to me.'

'Small. Drunk. A fornicator.'

'He sounds ideal. And you sound biblical. So does he.'

'Just fact,' I say.

When we appoint him on that premise, I tell him, 'No need for hostility between us. Though Petra – who you know – is furious.'

And he replies, 'You could have gone a long way with Petra. Hell and back.'

She wasn't Muslim. If there is an opposite, that was she. I say, 'I love the idea of Islam. Like going home. A home I've never been to.'

Harry says, 'You don't understand – and that we don't allow,' and suddenly he's talking in the name of our establishment, and sees me as a misfit. I look at his shoes for reasons, but they are middle range, and don't give much away.

I sit, dreaming of Khiva, where I've never been: the market, Tajiks in caftans, melons piled like bombshells, grain is maybe mixed with sand and gravel, but gravel from what sites! – the watchtowers, minarets, the bones of Russian soldiers, pearls abandoned.

Then I remember the old hippie road down to the south, guys good and bad seeking their gurus and settling, maybe, for a quick fumble in the fields and then – a generation of regrets and self-exclusion, American politics biting back, the hippies' hair now gone completely, the old Afghan coats turned back to camel skins.

And then – epiphany! No, tea is not strategic goods – the tea routes running up from India, along from China, then westward, northward, nice cuppas as the camels tire, a piece chipped off the brick, somehow the water's boiled, way above the Cold Mountains – then, suddenly, the clouds, my clouds, lift off – it's drugs! No tea, but poppies, magic this and that. Drugs for sure is strategic goods, and runs through all our continents.

I bring my discovery to Skullface, 'It was all a trick! My duties weren't for tea, but all these other substances,' and so he laughs, 'Well, Stag, you've got there, halfway at least. It doesn't matter what the stuff is, tea or smack. The routes, the carriage trade – that's where the interest lies, and who skims what, and who protects and sells, and what they buy and who they kill. But drugs is just hypothesis that serves. When guys get tired of freaking out, they'll turn to something else – maybe it's atom bombs, maybe it's sex – the thing is, are the roads policed, the caravans all mustered?'

'I feel cheated. And more central. And this means the nomads are again our vital source.'

'Your nomads, Stag! It could be anyone, a you, a me, we saddle up our mules, or camels, reindeer, and set off, find the pass, boil up our tea, and there you have it. Disaster only if we find some smart guy's made the stuff from chemicals. But since they haven't managed to replace tea, we think the drug trade will go on the same, unless they try to make it legal – but that spoils the fun, it stops transgression in its tracks, and all those cops and mafias – it all stops. And we are for free trade, young Stag, forget your humanistic glimmer there, join up! – it's trade that pays your wage and future hopes.'

Well, it's an argument.

Drugs! How banal. For a man of destiny. Pushing snot up the nose, a pipe of this, transfusion of that. Little spurts of pleasure, give a boost to the party, even a little fine writing in the skull. And my dream caravans? All quite irrelevant, the real business done with Toyotas, the VW Minibus, trekking the stuff and people over the holy roads, full of the aspiring hopeless.

My team – Popov and Anna, beautiful losers both – at least that Major Cai's got officer grade, though little else save hallucinations. And better far my voices, Afasian and Beest, my ministers of speed and intrigue – at least they feel the coolness of the keyboard, moments of pause before they write to me.

Old Skullface says of Popov, 'It's always better when you must decide to put on your horns and pitchfork, to be the pricker, not the pricked – even if that makes you somewhat of a prick!' and how he laughs, and adds, 'Well, Stag, so much for social revolution.'

'There must be something more than getting round the rules,' I say, but in the end I'm not convinced, and surely Cai and Anna won't support me, nor will Popov, now the cops have taken over his whole corporation, and his arsenal too.

Skullface is agitated, 'Stag, maybe your worldly wisdom can find a way to help me out ... I sent a thing for auction, thinking it to be a fake, they sold it but the buyer had it vetted. Now they've given him his money back, and I'll have nothing, and the firm now asks me thousands – costs of a valuation, enormous.'

'I think you'll have to pay them,' I say. 'You signed up for the game, you were in bad faith, a scam that failed.'

He sniffs, but this damned auction and its thousands, scam upon scam, runs through all our histories, like a golden thread, now until the end. It has become his life, his Personal Card.

*

Upstairs, the Institute is fine. The little conference rooms, the magazines all up-to-date, no sound from life below. But then you take the stairs – down, then past the Industrious Apes – it's what we call the monkeys, just for flattery – the wolves with their mechanical intelligence, opening doors and climbing trees – then poor dogs who can't do either, waiting for their master's hand. The pot-heads, singing in the locked room; further down, the mathematicians working out the probabilities, selling them on to television – price of diamonds, revolt in Saudi, melting of the ice and forests, discoveries of butterflies in Montreal – the planet skewing, lurching along, a top that's starting to run out of twist – the little human figures, their big heads dreaming of dinosaurs as heirs, yet procreating always, hoping for the best, counting their days, and days to come. Peeking at the ending, finding out who done it, and to whom. It's no surprise that Skullface thinks in terms of days: a day of peace, maybe to fix another auction, cut his loss.

I talk cautiously to Harry. He is the spy of spies, concerned with our security, but really with our every detail. When I count my friends and enemies, I never include him. He can always say whatever he thinks, because we daren't repeat it – it may be just a hook to fish us in. He says, 'We must do something with all these peoples, clans, these faiths and syncretisms. Tidy them all up, fit them in categories – monotheists, transcendentals, then the politicals – strongarms and weak, the ones who do and those who supplicate. Otherwise, it's chaos. All these mini-peoples when the rest of us are making out with women of all stripes, our children living in a broth of cultures, the first-round wives with secondary kids. American mums with Indonesian granddads.'

He turns to me and asks, 'Well, Stag, what's your take?'

'I love all these peoples, people, superficially,' I reply. 'I see them on their rounds, picking through old clothes, selling uncertain batteries, fighting for some dignity in the modern soup,' but Harry's quite the schoolman, hobnobs with categories and shades of inference. He ought to love himself a little more, just like the rest of us.

When we finish, Skullface is lurking there, OK, that's his job as well, to overhear, controlling the controllers, and later on, Harry is boasting of his conquests – not as a sliding from one conquest, one dissatisfaction, to another, but mountains climbed or animals bagged and trophied. Women! He tells me, 'This girl from Isfahan – the best. That false ingenuousness, skin like fresh mushrooms – highest quality,' and so and so, and on and on.

And later, we are wordless in his office, and I see a tall sad monkey in a corner of the room. He's urinating peacefully, and I think – he shouldn't be up here. They're not quite friends and not quite servants, but we have to treat them right, the work they do's industrial, though they are fed to make mistakes – a billion mistakes, in which the truth is latent, set like zircons.

'Hey, you!' shouts Harry.

The monkey turns in silence, ambles out, and Harry races after him, his boots are waving wildly, and I think, he shouldn't do it, he should be living, and letting us live our precariousness, a few more grey anonymous days, but he is off, his anger burning like a fire and ever higher, near to the stairs that go down to monkey planet, their property.

There is a 'frush', a sound of falling clothes and boots, a shout of 'Ape perdition', scutter of derisive paws ...

*

Skullface is philosophical. 'A frontline colleague, he was always close to death – for us, and now his passionate urge that brought to women of all creeds intense – maybe ephemeral – pleasure, and their kids no doubt some presents here and there – pursuing nature at its most suspect and hostile, tangling with the monkeys, has tumbled down the ladder of descent ...' he has lost the thread.

He wants to say that Harry is martyr to the cause, rather than to his anger, but the words are pallid and he breaks it off, we're all relieved and yet suspicious. No-one has fallen down those stairs before, and maybe Skullface with some silken twine ... or even the girl from Isfahan, who's maybe trained a monkey to do serious tricks ... And then I know, it must be Skullface, with his fear that Iranians are infiltrating everywhere, and surely Harry stumbled over the lines of duty, and I too must watch my step, a detour from the tea to drugs – the census of the risky traffics – skirting Iran, for now, and I'm for now, relieved.

I look at Popov, Anna and dear Cai, and think how risky is the promenade beneath the clouds, up where the glacier starts, a single step may last a thousand years, refrigerated.

*

A few days later, I see a monkey coming up the stairs – usually they're busy with robotic tasks. He holds a sheaf of papers, and I take it from his hand. He looks me in the eye. They're supposed to salute us, but he doesn't. I don't report him. Maybe he reports me for the lapse. It's hard to say if this is freedom – freedom for him, – if he's enjoying it. I see my logo on the dossier – a deer, a stag, looking backwards over its shoulder.

The dossier reads like a dialogue between two stand-up hams. 'He's either very stupid or well trained. When he was on Mount El'brus, all that mattered was the mountain. And he was wearing sneakers, so he's scarcely alpine.'

'Didn't he do some politics, while he was there? What does Popov say about it?'

'Well, there was a swarm of greens and Trots, odd commies and some pacifist guys and gals, freaky, and all with skills at entryism.'

'All Stag was interested in was folk music, drink, and women.'

'But that's the region where there's wars and industries of war.'

'He didn't seem to notice that, the factories, work-shops where they fix the tanks.'

'And yet he sought out some old trade unionists, guys on both sides, old sweeties, servants from the Soviet times.'

'Trying to contact oppositions, then. Clever!'

'Everything's been infiltrated, but he found a man who'd had his legs cut off, spent time with him.'

'But everyone's got thick dossiers on them, here ...'

'Well, remember, once he'd been on a march, and signed that letter.'

'Ah yes, that letter, some liberal squawk, so out of place, though one could understand his beef – but then again, it doesn't seem to fit the person.'

'Ingenuous and stubborn. Qualities to make him a public figure.'

Then a note, aside, 'Could employ as clever asset,' and another hand puts in, 'Query protection from a major power, and clearly trained – start him on tea,' and then 'mini-promote him into drugs'.

The report goes on, '... no political involvement of any kind, indifferent to the signs of conflict and of faith – interest in buying rugs and grave goods. But then – that woman bit him, maybe she had prised open the cover he was wearing – and wow she had wolf eyes.'

And the other comedian says, 'The Caucasus is full of wolves who've turned into women, vice versa too. D'you know why she bit him?'

''cos he wouldn't play.'

'I'm not convinced about his guru's wife – the one they say was acrobat, they say perhaps she was the most significantly dangerous woman in the Western world.'

'Naw, just mistaken identity. She didn't have a double life, forget the acrobat-housewife, they're two persons, separate from birth.'

'Well, someone's got to've been the most dangerous.'

'Confusion of names, forget it.'

I wonder who's been checking on me, maybe it's my best friend, but since I don't have one, who in hell …

I leave the file on Skullface's desk, and later hear him laughing over it as he must have done with all suchlike, and later Anna joins him and I hear complicit giggling. Ah, beautiful Anna. But all in all I haven't come out bad, career is forming – just that Cai and all that Chinese thought and such, they say the writing started as if monkeys thought it up (and how that Chinese delegation fumed when I suggested that!) – and oh my passion for the boss's Anna, servant to his human side, as if I cared, as if he had a human side. But I have my team online, economist, that's Beest and politologist, Afasian, and if I keep the monkeys sweet and don't offend, maybe I'll get the cash to travel further east, maybe the Cold Mountains, even.

And as I muse, I hear old Skullface bellow, 'The Iranians!' and of course he spots the missing element, the civilisation in between – between my Yuri Popov and the major Cai, that sweet and bitter bandit queen. Iranians. What are they doing in our ethnic soup, not quite astride our tea routes, certainly not immune from drugs – and yet my dossier does not mention them, and nor do I (remember Harry!) – and are they there, an absent presence, if not why not ... And at least they'll want to analyse the sheds where tanks are fixed and fitted up.

'Iranians,' I hear him whisper, 'Yon Stag was seeking something, must have been, when he climbed the mountain,' and Anna pitches in, 'Or was driven up it in a car,' and Skullface says, 'Yes, yes – the wolf that didn't bark, the bitten biter bit – and Petra now, it's clear – a loner tries to leave a sign, a message,' and I feel my scar and wonder what perversity it is that makes me long to be back in that bar, the covert brandy, nearly-dervish music, and Petra with her yellow eyes ...

*

I overhear Skullface: 'Yes, our friend's a little 'Turkish', you understand ... yes, yes, sympathies are good, but in that respect – to send him round the world, chatting to presidents, what's the good? No, first he must do boot camp, somewhere tough to make his name, maybe accomplish what we need.'

For us, overhearing is the most important of the arts, the attested means of communicating. Does he mean to send me to the jungle or the desert, even to the mountains, and I'm torn – the great dilemma, become a public figure or be what I want? I think of all the armed militias, battalions of irregulars everywhere, anonymous fighting, armies of widows training on rope walls, of armed resistance in the Thirties in the forests of Ukraine, of horrible people living ordinary miserable lives, of ordinary people doing horrible things, and not regretting, moving along. Of people living in narrow boundaries, expecting rebirth and so quite smug, or now, uncertainty removed, just knowing it's just once, this life.

And here is Popov, so I ask, 'How was it, all of you, moving on to your next history lesson – blood on your hands, perhaps?'

*

Anna and Cai sneak in, they use my office as a listening post, while Popov says, 'No blood on my hands! We have a special soap,' and Cai's amused and says, 'Maybe it's guilt, and you should tell us why,' and Popov points to me and says, 'Poor guy, you, Anna rode him like a horse,' and lightening things up I say, 'Old Skullface seems to have a deal with our monkey friends.'

I'm always courteous when mentioning them, you never know, and Cai puts in, 'Well, he's responsible for them, the pity is, those monkeys never will grow up. Or talk to us,' and Anna adds, 'Or know the finite,' and we all reflect and think the monkeys have it good. I don't know what to say.

'I have to do my sums,' I say. 'The traffic in those drugs and other things, and even people, seems hotting up. Starting poor just makes you quite insatiable,' and Cai concludes the thought: 'for cash', and we are quiet and contemplate, and think of Anna's life with George and how he died, and maybe too we think of Harry. And Cai says, 'We don't even know if that girl from Isfahan was real or not,' and I tell them, 'Anyone can have an imaginary girl with skin that's like fresh mushrooms – but then, those military men like Harry, they've bonded hard in tents with other men. Perhaps our Harry was inclined to other things – he sure as hell reacted to that monkey' – 'who someone planted in his room,' adds Cai.

She tells us how they made them change their houses, that once they lived in courtyards with the women on one side. The spacious farms were rubbled, then the animals were confiscated, everyone went to hi-rise living, and the old respect made no more sense, but she surely misses the old times with the chickens and the goats and privacy, the gates were shut and they were all inside with all they loved and hated, not like now, where who knows what lies underfoot and dancing in the night above and maybe murder in the next apartment. And we are silent, thinking of times all swept away, how sad that Anna should have only George, a shadow if not quite a ghost, still lingering on, bit of her identity that serves for absolutely nothing, all those hormones gone to waste, and how it makes her such a bore, and bitter with it, never letting go but nothing, really, to cling on to ... But in different ways both she and Cai have something I could suffer for, some sentiment. If I were humanist, or even a philosopher, like Cai's incinerated one! The man is burnt, the book lives on but no one has a clear idea of what it means and signifies, for after all, if it's just about a building plan, well, we don't care, the walls have tumbled down, sown with blood and lime and spit, and so life passes on and by and maybe up. Arriving at banality, I say, 'I guess we're all in some human condition', Cai laughs and says, 'Well, after all, you are just what you say,' and Anna says, 'I hardly speak at all,' and we all laugh, and Popov tells us, as he leaves, 'One thing you can accept, that when the boss of bosses speaks, you better jump,' but that's the thing the boss is waiting to overhear, an insincere but ingratiating gesture. And so he leaves, Cai grieving for her courtyard home, Anna for George, and me for the confusion of the clans that if you try to taste and touch it, burns you. And I touch my scars.

Old Skullface calls me in. He is excited, even smiles. 'We've the idea,' he says, 'To change our name, from INSTITUTE OF POSSIBILITIES to INSTITUTE OF PROBABILITIES. The TV sales are going well, none of our hypotheses is overturned. And then there's plans for you.'

Through the window I see a pair of arms, a bottom and a tail, and then another.

'I thought the monkeys hunkered down at night,' I say, 'right by their desks, but now I see them swarming over us, even to the roof,' and he replies, 'The new regime, dear friend. I let them out for exercise, a pity that we don't have one of those old buildings with the insides out, so they could climb up pipes and wires and such,' again he smiles. I think of Anna.

'It gives us time, if needs be, to check their laptops,

sort the devils out,' he means the aliens that lie in wait, the virus in the software.

'More tasks for them,' he says. 'Seeking the life meanings, takes a bit of time, of patience,' and he sighs, Napoleon waiting for his second or his third coming or going. 'Of course, we only try to change the surface of things, the rest is genocide or worse, things quite reprehensible, as I agree. Stick to the surface, Stag Delfine.'

'Avoid the teflon, then,' I joke, but he is high, and running like a train:

'My friend, our Popov showed you how the world is interleaved and tall, I might say hierarchical,' and he pauses as if taking in a mountain yet unclimbed.

'And you are still, I fear, a zero. But inflatable.'

He leans back. More monkeys rise and fall, and some look in and show their teeth – a grin? Contempt? Or just the strain of clinging on.

'A crew', he says: 'Those primal things that's hard to discipline,' and I think of the urinating monkey, of Harry's fall.

'Sometimes they forget themselves, but after all, we can't have these Iranians infiltrating here – besides, a military man should know his days are numbered, that is why he sets his mark upon the document that says, "We may at any time, for any reason, snuff you out." For that is duty, Stag, and patriotism, although the words sound quite banal, if not archaic.'

And he goes on: 'I'd so much hoped you'd find a spot of quiet with that young Cai, we try to fit our operatives up, but you are both – it seems to me – prisoners of old thinking: she has to be, she's nothing else, they've nothing much to do but walk about and try forgetting that quite frantic past. And shop. But you, I fear – your mind is solid rock, fixated on that time before the time before, you can't let go a fantasy of what is gone and never was. Take me, and Anna. Her, I do respect,' and he goes on about her past, adventures with that guy, and how he's happy with her now, they even cook some pancakes after making love, he's quite a skilful chef, and on he goes, and all those words and images, and this and that and stuff, and Anna is the prize. How he has dealt with sponsors – everyone, it seems – the corporations, states, the dissidents, transgressors, anyone who wants a list of sums and goods and possibilities – maybe in the end he makes a little shipment – of this and that. I hope it's guns not drugs because, though death is all the same with both, indeed with anything at all, at least the guns is action, though the pain involved is sharper and not transitory.

Anna's the prize, for what, for who, I wonder, what are her gifts? He says, 'Maybe she can get things fixed, supply escapes, or improvise a cure. She has the gift of being quite indifferent to right, and what's the other thing,' he laughs, 'She'll get you out of there, wherever, find a boat, a helicopter. Fix that thing.'

And I'm so pleased, my secret is my secret team, the guys that no one knows, advice that I've not solicited, but surely they'll be there, and if I need, they'll make the situation. Anna will pick me up.

I say to Skullface, 'There's more cops outside.'

He peers out, seeming to ignore the monkeys: 'No, just the usual, cruising for lunatics.'

He describes my project. He is a kingmaker. I am not a king. He is godlike. But he's not a god. He says, 'You'll find yourself, well, with street people.'

'It's all the same to me.'

'No, not the same. You must have love, commitment. Or else it's not for you.'

We pause. He says, 'You'll see them as ordinary, guys that's even lost. But in the jungle, forest, desert, they must seem saviours, inspirers, our absent Venuses, Apollos.'

Again a pause. 'Philosophically speaking, that's the point. Love. And you see, just speaking. But as for your intentions? Accomplishments? All states, all movements – all have dirty hands. So, love, where does that come in? You must love, not see or speak. Then your intentions turn to history, to all kinds of facts. Love not for country, and not right or wrong, but for suffering.'

I object, 'But why should these guys – some kinds of combatants I guess – want peace, even for a day?'

He says, 'Once, I was in Moscow. Some show, some speech – in Soviet times. Why was I there? Who knows, maybe like you I won a bet. And maybe you remember, the war in Vietnam?'

'I've seen it mentioned.'

'Well, it was in full swing. And there came a delegation from the North, in uniform. You remember, everyone pretended the regulars weren't involved, but there they were. And triumphantly, when they came in we all stood up, to honour them. Who knows what all the others present felt? All I know is that for me, they were the heroes, victors – and I was filled with love for them. We, all big bristly westerners, our faces carcase colour, and they were tiny, out of our world. Fighting our fight. Not left or right, but epic.'

'A bad war, as I remember.'

'Unspeakable. But at that point we didn't think of deaths, reprisals, afterwards – and I say "we" though maybe I was all alone. It was a war that had to be, as natural as growing up.

'And this epiphany has stayed with me, this sense of species being, solidarity, indifferent to logic. When you go to island or to jungle, where the cover is magnificent – the trees that reach the stars, the animals all furred and multicoloured ...'

I interrupt: 'These street people, then – a new ruling class, alert to their fellows' needs?'

'I wouldn't bet on it. We're not monkeys, Stag. We own more stuff, for one. But we can't manage our destiny. That's what we call our freedom. Your mission, though, is to support these fighters, blindly. Objectively. Because we know there's always injustice and misery, and that states hide it, cause it, and when they concoct a remedy, they're like the rich man who brings prosperity maybe to many, but above all, first of all, to himself. You make life in the interstices, but to do so you must hide the great fault of the species. We are cruel and selfish, Stag. I no less than you. Not my discovery, of course.'

He is in full flood. 'Wealth is a bet on the future, like the bet that took me to Moscow. And all that's been swept away. And was it all unjust, I ask? And is what comes thereafter, is that all fun and lollypops? We are all historians of the future, Stag. Avant la letter,' and he laughs, mispronouncing.

I think of my adventure up the mountain. And did I love the clans that lay beneath, that hate each other, though to a tranquil eye they all seem interchangeable?

And Skullface, trying to ingratiate himself, has taken steps to distance everything from logic. Love, or blind faith? Or blind obedience. It all comes to the same.

I ask Skullface, 'And my duties with the drugs?

What's to become of them?'

Abstractedly he says, 'Drugs? Drugs, we all take drugs, to live a longer and a happier life – we hope no one gets killed or impoverished assisting us. And Stag, the big thing now is water. And air, naturally. The rest is marking time, it's physiological. And are your motives always, really, truly humanist? Although you say you aren't. And what is humanism anyway? Vain hopes, dear friend, that all may live as you when you live well, and when you don't, a pox on them. Besides, when you are in the forest, on the plain, those warrior guys are like the ancient mercenaries, their value ends if they get killed, and so they live for war, but fight as little as they can. And then fight dirty.' And he sniggers.

I'm impressed by Skullface's pragmatic revolutionism. It comes from some younger self, or creature, that flourished before he reached the bosses' office.

Skullface muses, 'Of course, clans are much more,' he stares at me, 'Sticky. Than families or nations – course, there is a downside too. Think of the Georgian,' and I think of Anna's George, the dead Georgian, brought out, jangly skeleton, when she wants to dump a suitor.

'Think of Stalin, all his nonsense – zapping the cousins even unto the third degree, anathema the marriage without the boss's sayso, all that superfluous blood and guts. Stag, you know about clans, and Cai does too, salt of the earth – but also scum, and when you think of families, those awful sulky kids, and nations, all those flags for burning, silly uniforms, just like operetta, and that stuff about one for all and all for one when all we want is skipping military duty, maybe the taxes too ... ah, my dear friend, and now they spring it on us – a planet in its death-throes, we've all to join some super ant colony, each happy with its lot, though maybe also cannibal, and we pull together, pull like a team of goats – against another team ...'

Anna's come in to hear the ending. We stare at him, then at each other, and Anna says – we don't quite know what she thinks – 'In a pig's eye', and maybe it's agreement, or a sign to shut old Skullface up, and yes, it's all our job, but also not a concern of ours, and so we stare out through the window at that wide sky, though, true, it is a bit discoloured, but who cares, and when it rains it's still a goddam nuisance, and I think again of shoes and their protection from the weather, and it's time to go, it's all a bit obsessive, that won't do, except that most of what we do's obsession, call it routine and values, coming home to the correct address, waving the cultural flag, find someone who'll fight for us, defend our civilisation ... a line of verse comes into mind as we get off the elevator: 'It's life ole friend,' and Skullface says, 'Look at poor Stag, there – off in the Caucasus again, I'll bet, and looking for another bite to even that one up,' and they all laugh, as if my scars have made me real, but all they've done is set a question, another, maybe, love, or maybe just the usual tedium with claws.

Life in the Forest

BENEATH, there is a map of green and brown, with maybe monkeys interlaced in trees, perhaps there's desert, pink stone flowers, a rusty pickup's bones, extent of squalid nothing, bits of nature lying there, unloved, unloving.

I'm with the fighters. We don't discuss what they are fighting for, it seems it should be quite self-evident. I josh along with their big chief, he calls himself Apollo. We spend some time on neutral ground, on women. Common folklore. I say, 'I'd quite like a relation with Cai – might do her good,' and laugh. Apollo says, 'Men look for women who will hurt them. So that in turn they can be bad to them.' And laughs.

At least I hope she isn't turned, like Daphne, into a bush. He says, 'Of course, we take your mythic names, though not their powers.'

His view of life is simple – they have to face opponents' strategy of Provocation followed by Punishment. The big powers, when they're winning, drive you to the wall, and then pick off the margins. Then get the compromisers to hit their feisty brothers, make the feisty ones turn fratricide. The word is always peace, the policy is war.

I say, 'Apollo,' and feel so stupid naming him, that he too smiles, reacts in slow time, and I go on, 'Is it true there's a mail service leaving here?' and he replies, 'Sure we communicate – that's our job' and then I hear from Skullface in two days. He writes:

'First, your tea assignment. That special brew, fermented, that made them millions in the boom – is bust,' and since it went the length of China, made me think the room was there for opium wars, and then old Skullface warns, 'And spare me comments on the food, young Stag, the washing and the animals, fever, music and the rest. What interests me's the military side, and only that,' and I think that that's too bad, for all we have to talk about is what we eat, spaghetti and canned okra, hear the only tape they have – that goddam skunk metal band. They've shown me what they read – an anthology of Bakunin, Marx being out of date they say, and an extra is a pamphlet by Cai's old burnt philosopher – on how the sciences are really music of the spheres, construction done by choral singing.

And it takes me months to realise that Apollo reads what I have sent, replies in my, or anyone's name. And then I let the fever take me.

*

It is in a vision that I see my old mate Popov dangling from a tree, with some great beast, chimera or crocodile, that's climbed the trunk and taken off his foot. And now my guys have bound him up and filled him with more dope, because he seemed quite high when snagged up in the tree, and now the beast has loped off somewhere – usually the animals here, inedible, are big as squirrels, maybe a flying badger, nothing extraordinary. And I ask him what he came to do, ungrateful.

'How can a spy work with a limp?' he says to cheer me up, though he's sure sad to lose his foot. His state will never pay him off for that, and here it's hopeless, as they're all high on Bakunin and self-help (although it seems to me that what they want is State to help them out of state's embrace) – but now I'm stuck with Popov, who can't run.

And all we seem to do is listen to the radio – they tell us that patrols are coming, and our guys fire some rounds at backsides in the bush, then it's our backsides are bolting up the hill, and all our stuff is lost or scattered, and our breath is scarce as water.

So I hope the next time will be Anna, who is skilled at rescuing, if at nothing else. Though why they want to rescue me when planting me was such a task, I cannot think.

*

Life in the forest is pleasant. If it were not for the terror of instant death, or capture, and being beaten about, it's almost a healthy life. The food is one of the hardships I'm forbidden to mention and in any case would be the same whatever my complaints. We have reverted to the condition of a warrior band. Since we are the hunted, not the hunting, when we feel safe we laugh and sing, and even when we're under threat I try to chant beneath my breath.

Although Apollo sees me as a winning card – old Skullface must have promised something – I must not be taken prisoner, or that would blow the whole game, so I'm at a loss what I should do if running doesn't save us.

At times we shoot, at times we read the book, and someone gives their thoughts but not too much. The others have a history that's sent them here, like history it makes them what they are, but there's no point in telling how – the torture, death, the frameup, loss of dignity or something worse.

I say to Rama, who I think of as the Thug, 'They say revenge is sweet, but also eaten cold, we're used to that, since here we can't light fires and try it hot,' but my come-on doesn't loosen him. He says, 'We'll know what to do with them!' which is predictable, but adds, 'Of course, we must select, for after all, it doesn't help to promise bloodbaths, whatever the moral case may be,' and warrior Hector says, 'The killing and a battle's different things. I'd want no part in retribution, however you can justify it,' but I think that all this talking, maybe the thinking too, amounts to very little.

And as I think of what old Skullface wants, and how my 'day of peace' might seem to warriors running for their lives, a message comes: the girl who's selling 'weeks', it may be months, of peace – a rival plan – is making ground. And so my stay will shortly end.

I try to put Apollo at his ease. His name is larger than his body, certainly than his face. I say, 'At Rhodes they drove a four-horse chariot into the sea in your name and honour. You, the invincible companion. You who rise and fall, or set,' and he laughs:

'With rising and falling, that puts me between the Wild Boys and the Mild. But you are right, yes, I do believe the past is co-determinate with our times, the gods indeed our companions. And where the roses grow without a limit, there I was honoured. Maybe just my name,' and I'm alarmed, for I see his namesake may take him on a rant, which I'd join in, but I'm scared of putting my feet wrong, joining that chariot in the sea.

I wonder, did they bring the horses back, this habit of expensive sacrifice seems to divide these old guys from us moderns, but then I think of shooting rockets at the moon and making tapes of lice on Venus, and I think maybe we too know how to spend and overspend. We have to spend a buck to show we know a thing or two on how the universe is ordered – gods and sirens, nymphs and all kinds of creeping things that visit us by night, alas it isn't Anna, nor yet Cai. More likely Beest with patent papers to be signed.

Who knows what interest there is in these shabby assisted warriors, in what they think? It's all provisional, so long as we are battling in the scrub. I know we must be observable from space, the rusty cans alone must shine like tiny stars, they all know where we are, so do they wait to kill us one by one, or just a-simmering here?

Apollo says, 'I have to get the questions and the answers sorted out, although these bombs and bullets shake my concentration on the language front. Meanwhile, Delfine, your presence gives us some protection,' and I see that Skullface, if he doesn't run the show, at least determines how it all works out, the times and rhythms. Probabilities department stacking up our chances, discovery of some resource that makes us worth more than the Wild Boys – they have nothing but their rhetoric – and the Mild Boys, the sweet smell of their sacrifice.

I say, 'I often think the people involved are not the ones we – they – thought they were.'

*

Apollo laughs. 'We change our shape. But I am still the invincible, the African, sun. And why does violence trouble you, and not, say, poverty, which hurts you all your life?'

I say, 'It's a personal, not an analytic thing.'

'And why a day of peace? Why not find someone who'll push it for a week? A month? It's all the same to me, or rather, if it works, then I can wait. We can't think in terms of days or weeks.'

I think how Skullface is a modest type. The others – they have just ideas and plans, and need for still more others to play the parts that need a sacrifice of flesh and blood. While he just starts it off and waits.

I must go delicately, I say, 'Bakunin gives you extreme flexibility. *Extreme*.'

He is not pleased. 'That's the beauty, and the plague. After all, we don't do this to become theologians.'

I recall, 'Wasn't it peasants and revolution? Then trade unions? Reforms? Direct action? Propaganda by the deed, a bomb to hasten it along.'

He dismisses this. 'These are strategic options, yes, that in time were taken, mostly wanting.'

'As solutions to whatever problems, I'd say largely zero.'

'Because they failed, because the people weren't prepared. Or else were overwhelmed.'

I let this circulate. I hope Rama and Hector don't start in with their objections, which often end in beatings. I regret starting these limping hares.

Apollo says, 'These old books lead to old arguments. First you feel the goad, the wind, the flame, they bear you up. Then maybe a book, to give you weight,' and I add, 'To drag you down.'

He repeats, 'Who wants to be a theologian, who knows what those religious freaks may have in mind? And they're as flexible as us. Or perhaps there comes some continuity, some figure who gives it all a shape, interpretation. Then into battle, and it all transforms. Or even some success, new guys come in, they've new objectives...'

I'm quite surprised. 'I've seen you for a while, quite determined and coherent, braving the worst and doing it, and now you make it all seem relative.'

He turns away and says, 'We want quite well defined, quite other things. As do the Mild, the Wild. You have to learn the language, Stag.'

And I think of Skullface and his aliens, and who knows what they want, it's certainly not to sit in forest clearings eating okra with a spoon from cans. Although he has his monkeys, they sure as hell do what he wants and stand there po-faced, well drilled and tails neat curled to left or right, and not a sneer or eyebrow out of place.

I can't tell Skullface about the hardships, which is most of our life here. And the military part is just the normal time of fearing death. We are only one group, maybe not the toughest, not the most skilful – there are the Wild Boys and the Mild Boys. The Mild Boys want to take over government. The Wild Boys have some religious plan, some interpretation of some book – like we have, but a weightier one – they want redemption, not just liberation, then off down a pleasanter track. Redemption leads you to some pre-existing truth, which quite diminishes what you might accomplish.

But I am sure that none of us is making arms and gunpowder, so someone somewhere trucks it in, and in a way they're making sure that we go on, and even send up cans of okra – wonder what the other guys are eating, and I hear the religious ones have steak, or maybe it is made from leaves or bark, but goddam okra's one thing for breakfast that you wouldn't want. And knowing as I do that I lack all passion and conviction, we're back to hardship, and there's no reward, and as for peace and war, I say to Apollo: 'I guess it's all just tit for tat, and nothing about causes and effects – the means for peace and all its purposes are really just like those for war,' and he replies, 'Your day of peace is just publicity. A day, a month, a year. Developing a taste for peace or reconciliation – well, Stag, that's always there, or somewhere round.'

And so I think: 'Then Skullface is a devil, or at least a devil's advocate.'

Apollo laughs. 'You can't think your Skullface is behind us?'

'Not exactly.'

'If we must put up with you, we must get something in return, of course. And we may move into towns. It's horrible here.'

'Can you so easily change shape?'

'Yes.'

'More corruption, more contacts,' I say. 'And the peasants?'

'Peasants want more land, at first to work on, then to sell, to rent, to use as guarantees. When they've nothing, then they're on our side, but afterwards ...'

'But to restore autonomy, the purity? The whole pre-modern dream?'

'Are you instructing us?'

'I wouldn't dream ...'

'Besides,' he says, with force, 'I don't exactly see you praying ...'

'I pray all the time.'

'For yourself – and anyway, all this military stuff, hardly pre-modern. Glory is what we need. The ancient glories and a stronger hand in bargaining,' and we both look at the long ridge of scrub beyond the camp, the okra cans, some things that look like ape bones.

'Well, I'm a sceptic,' I say. 'Not too observant – and not political.'

'Well, Major,' he says with wasted irony, 'How'd you escape the politics, when you're part of it?'

I make a noncommittal sound. And think of Cai – she's known that politics is everything, the music, houses, goats and chickens, and I think to console myself, that if it's everything it's also nothing and invisible like air, we need it only when it's ceased to be, and maybe old Bakunin saw it right although for when and who I cannot say, nor can Apollo and the rest.

Apollo says, 'Our power comes from your reaction,' and I think, 'He's not been long in his job, because this idea draws him along. Then Rama grasps the initiative – the action – from it. The idea's a motor, not realisable even in myth or epic, just a force. Comprehensible – but all that killing ...'

Afasian says, 'Remember your history,' but which particular one? And he's no guide – it's politics, and so – it's discourse off the cuff, or serpentine. And Mr Beest communicates, he says, 'Haha, you've got a goldmine there, all you need is miners ...' and it's something Apollo seems to recognise.

He says, 'That Personal Card of his, it just requires a special stone. And here, from all the world, we're sitting on a load of it. *The* load of it.'

I think, 'We are all like these stones.'

We are none of us being sincere.

Apollo is hard as these stones, and so is Rama – but Rama likes cruelty, and though his name means exotic adventures and difficult victories, through inspiration he's become more or less a thug. And Hector's just a warrior.

I know, but I don't care, how they can use these stones, and fit them into little spy shells to carry round and lie, as if all culture was not a lie, like clothes, and all the things that make us more ingratiating, and more dangerous than the monkeys at headquarters.

I don't care, because we've all lived with guerrillas and the state guerrillas, nationalist states and nationalist liberators. Our neighbours and ourselves – we all talk freely of freedom and punishment, of doing down the different and being them. As Skullface says, we know about hardships, they bore us, the people who're behind the people, we think we know the plotters as we plot, we think that influence is nobler than the deed itself. That's what thought is, itself and round the back again.

And now Apollo lets me stay, because old Skullface gave him something so he would, but for me it's just an interlude before I mount old Skullface's stage, the one with all the presidents and ministers.

Apollo asks, 'Would you like to read my poetry?'

'No thanks.'

'It isn't just the sun that makes things grow, but poetry too. That takes you to the beginning.'

'Hmmm.'

He makes me read some. It is esoteric, manichean, even decadent. He is too large in them. He is liberator and also founder, nature wilts as he observes it, the animals stop their eating and their fighting and all their other things, as he observes them. He does not convince, but I have nothing other, nothing more nor less – for while I'm here, he's everything. Life, death, and more.

*

I send a note to Cai. 'These guys say they're anarchists – but they're just pros at the subversion game – flexibility for the possible. Somewhere between maximum and minimum, the artwork of the tossed bomb and the pastoral of the commune. Complicated search for simplicity. And your book, Cai, 'just connect' – well, so it is. Just look at our new resource, the stones. No laws written on them, just fortunes. We'll have the prospectors here in no time, our great new bargaining counters, like monster tiddlywinks. Which philosopher will be burnt this time, Cai?'

And Apollo, I notice, looks at me as if he knows he'll be the one to navigate this load of stones, make the alliances, pretend the bombs are really the careless lovely ones of centuries ago, bring it all down, rise up the free unfettered spirit. All that. Not deals, but purification. Hector could be quite pleased to see I call him 'warrior', but, well, Rama's just a thug, and maybe pleased with that, who cares.

I'm quite affectionate, thinking of our old institute, the monkeys patterning the old brown bricks with a golden interlacing, a mesh of arabesques, of paws and tails. Even old Skullface, surely just a naughty freak, and not the master of the games? And I forget poor Harry and the dreary tasks that wait for me – enthusing the presidents.

Cai says, 'The boss can put everything at risk. With that power, he could do everything and its contrary, and I'm afraid he will.'

I say, 'None of that nonsense about good boss, bad boss. He had his plan, but never countenanced transformation, never expected transcendence ...'

'But what he's managed with the monkeys is

remarkable.'

I remember the scenes with her – the dynamiters' ball – not exactly an adventure, but impressive all the same.

She says, 'Me being between two worlds, I think gives me some pervasive strength – belonging to your world which demands nothing of me, except total belief and loyalty, and losing mine – mine, where hatred and betrayal are the givens, given risks, maybe, but currency,' and I think I see us in a landscape, white as silver and a sky that's uniform enamelled blue – it's terribly cold. I think I see a wolf, poisoned perhaps, it climbs painfully into a tree, and on a leafless branch I see its mate is stretched out there – poisoned, both of them, I guess. In the distance there's a railway line, there's a toy train, carrying away toy people, maybe it's just far off, and there's a little covered station, a kind of shed, people are drinking here, and there's a man in pebble glasses, quite drunk, prone like a penitent, trying to support himself and move, two bright green gherkins in his hands, supporting him, little stumps, frail tiny crutches. I think, 'He looks he could be a poet', and I look for Cai and she's not there, and I feel angry, a great deafening anger, that she puts these visions in my head and then backs off, an exploitation of the – what? Imagination? Presence? I can do nothing for her, can't stop the carousing and the carousel, these people who seem very poor and desperate. Where before the drunks were capering, these are somnolent, near sleep or death, the train is tiny but it's not a toy, it takes a part of them away, the others just can't make it up its steps.

I say, 'Cai' – and surely, somewhere she can hear me, 'I know some things in motion can't be modified ... But where are you? Where is the something else we look for, expect to see,' and there is silence, and I know there's nothing to be said or done, though we will do and say it all again, and probably the Boss is doing well, to master squads of monkeys ... it must mean something, doing what he wills, or maybe being part of it.

But – hard to call this an adventure, and I'm just her instrument, for the nothing that she needs to say. Her past, her life, is done – beyond repair. So, what does she do now? Nothing I can tell her.

Rescue!

AND SUDDENLY, it's Anna, a little grubby but well kitted-out.

I say, after the greeting, 'Why are you here?'

'Rescue. My strong point.'

'They'll kill us if they see us. The others too will kill us if they see us.'

She is not disturbed. 'After your guys started to massacre, what's the point in staying?'

I object, 'Well, it's their job – or maybe just one aspect of it. And anyway, it was tit for tat.'

'That's a consolation, then,' she says. 'But follow that with a day of peace, and you'll be laughed to extinction. And besides, the other celebs came and got away unharmed.'

'That was before the killing. And they were sold – these guys can't be bothered with long kidnaps, they're on the move. They traded hostages for more supplies, and no harm done. But now, the stakes have risen ...'

She asks, 'Where's Popov – made the initiative to rescue you, but really to upstage the boss.'

'They had to trade him for some cans of carrots – diced – they couldn't stand his lamentations. You need an expert if you rescue someone.'

She repeats, 'It's my strong point,' and we manoeuvre ourselves to an inconspicuous place, more or less what I'd call some bushes.

'What's Skullface think about it all?'

She giggles, and I think of motels, with pancakes after. She says, 'If you didn't call him Skullface you might respect him more.'

I might. I might even love him, along with the other clans and warriors, my ephemerals – Afasian, the wandering Armenian who turns up everywhere, invoked or not, and Dr Beest, maybe a Hindu or just American, doing his sums to get a cap and gown. And shall I see them all again – though see is not quite the sense, sensation. In the laptop. Shall I log on to them, and maybe find if they have flesh? And surely I may see my friend, the mutilated Popov, see if he's really lost his foot, and Anna says 'Let's snuggle down behind these shrubs.'

Well, it was what I think I'd always wanted, though I prefer a situation where there's past and future, not just running and sudden death.

She says, 'It's time to make love, now. Out of our time, a space. I know that's what you want.'

And it was good with Anna.

It was not *very* good with Anna.

Her body's soft, but that tough mind is not quite pearl in oyster. Rather, you wonder if it's not the knife beneath the mattress.

In the morning, we slouch off – the sentry always sleeps near dawn. We're sticky in our sticky clothes. I ask, 'Where the hell are we going?' and she says, 'I've got some chums to meet us,' and I know she's done a deal, a fix made with the other side. 'If my guys get caught, they'll be exterminated,' I say, and she shrugs on, 'They should never have done that massacre. It changed the rules.'

And I protest: 'But you've become a player, now responsible for consequences far beyond just rescuing me – which could be done for cash, maybe a bazooka or some such.'

She says sternly, 'No more toys, Stag. They broke the pact, their cover's compromised, their friends at court have had enough. No more cash for tricky exploits. Their game is over, Stag – though yours has just begun.'

We run away. I wonder, 'Whatever happened to Bakunin?' – and yet the pretext for my guys' slaughtering was quite in line – the villagers were setting up a kind of state, they'd deviated. And all because their chief drank so much beer he couldn't judge the cases brought before him – so, instead of custom or rotation, the idea was to set up a committee, elections, ambassadors, all that stuff. And worst of all, no longer to act as intermediaries. So, no more messages and no more supplies, and even worse, a pact made with the capital. No more needful traffic.

And as we run, I see the other soldiers, cleaner than mine, and more afraid. I hear them mortaring my friends. Anna asks, 'What induced them to kill those villagers?'

Absurd to say, 'Bakunin made them do it.' I don't say, I don't think, 'frustration.' I say instead, 'Change in the balance of forces.'

I'm back. I pick up a paper. I've not yet been launched, I'm still anonymous speculation.

Here's something about me, SNEAKERING UP RUSSIA – must have been Cai that spread the news I mountaineered in sneakers. Popov wore his, but I – I, my fine Italian shoes. And here is one for Skullface, PROBE HARRY SNADDER'S FALL. This will be with us all our lives. It's true that I wore sneakers in the forest, not on the mountain, in the car – so how to set the story right?

Old Skullface beams, 'Well, all your tribulations over, now's the time to enjoy your prize,' and I think, 'I already had it,' and smile at Anna – though of course, old Skullface has his three-deck experiences with her, and he is still the boss, and what am I, who knows, and I don't care.

Celebrity

BEING A CELEBRITY is just what I expected. Most celebrities were something, had some talent, previously. All I had was the mountain. A view. Some hardships, now forgotten. Maybe, as they say, 'a take on life', a view from very high, the clans and dialects of the world. And now, try to reach conclusions, like peering in an engine, that's turning, spitting, turning.

I remember one of the presidents. He is quite distant. He cannot ask me what I am, and so he asks a spook he has to take around with him. 'The guy that parlayed with the terrorists,' I hear. And I don't even have a fresh tooth-mark to show for it.

The President brings himself back from somewhere. He's like a man who's juggling with six eggs – we know he'll drop some and so spoil his act, but he knows too to throw them high and higher, so the trick will last, they're in the air, and those of us who still have faith can wish him well and wait for all those eggs to change their colours, silver, purple, green, as they pass up and down before the lights.

He has a special wife, I wonder how he met her, standing there beneath the eggs, but maybe they get used to meeting people while they're juggling, or maybe some chief spook has joined them up to make a pair, a project. She's a celebrity too and no one now remembers what her talent was before she took to posing, perhaps she was a stripper or a medium, skier or princess, hard to tell, her clothes are never bought in stores, her body has been set in some particular boneshop, so you see a lot of spine and ribs, the rest is all stuck on abundantly, but she talks too, she doesn't stop, and gradually her body matters less, and you can watch her lips, out come the words, an engine turning, spitting, turning.

I interrupt. I say, 'I'm the guy that's bringing peace. That is, not bringing anything at all, but just the plan ...To stop them, us, doing what we're doing, so that there is nothing going on at all,' and she scents something, but he says, 'Ok, the terrorists, yes, so what's the good of peace with them?'

And I confess, there doesn't seem to be much there, but he goes on, 'Had some woman here the other day – now, she was for a month, or year, of peace – I can't remember which – a length of time you can do something with, stock up with guns, or buy the guys, or have them argue, who knows what. A day! It isn't worth a spit,' and to myself I must admit, he's quite a sharp old dear, he wears some medals, which the others don't. A stag retired from rutting but with many scars, and when he's dead I wonder what the wife will do, I guess she'll start the circle over, when the eggs have all come down she'll maybe make a soufflé, and I laugh, which isn't in the plan at all. And so he sees me as a lightweight, or more likely, a contemptuous type who sniggers – he turns again to his spook minder, and I hear, 'Iranians' and I wonder why this jealousy of someone else's culture, surely they should start to have one of their own, and I feel Petra's teethmarks, and I wonder if I'll ever see her, and so thinking, it is clear I won't. And better so.

The relation with the President's wife was like stepping into another, maybe a previous, century, more polite and expert. And discovering, through her, a different race of men. 'What's that smell', I wonder, 'Can it be patchouli, whatever that might be,' but she says it's the usual stuff that very expensive women wear. Her small talk too's minute, but in a fruity voice – what fruit, I wonder, maybe Chinese gooseberry – it seems immense.

'The chandeliers are held in place by screws through beams. They're washed with soap, though that is not my job,' she says. I see why caravans of drugs are needed as therapies for her. She clearly fancies me, or else I am part of her job, she stands so close, maybe in receptions there is such a crush you stand like this so you can hear, it means that her dress, so loose the label flaps, is just a curtain for her underwear, with every move it gapes, reveals. I want to say, 'You were a pro before the marriage, then,' but don't. I mean 'professional', but in this circle, woe if you're misunderstood. She takes my hand and here's a breast, somewhere beneath my shoulders, nestling in – it bears it's own uncoded message. Later, it seems, she leaves these parties more easily than all the rest of us who stand around, wanting to go, unknowing the procedure.

She is quite small, undressed, but her perfume, detached from her, is huge, it fills but does not rock the room, and as the phrases come to mind I giggle and that seems to spur her on.

'Well, Mr Peace,' she says, 'I hope you're not so peaceful now that we're alone,' and I think that this should be my line, but she has set her sails for love, or at least quick stripping off and clouds of dust and smell of cash rise up.

She seems to have a special contraceptive set, a kind of toolkit I have never seen before, I say, 'I don't think you'll need all that stuff,' but she is silent, and I suppose that in affairs of state a small mistake can fill the tabloids and TV for months and maybe more, and so she fits it up, and then we're in the next part of the test, and here it seems she's used to some performing men from cultures strange, unknown to me, I don't know how they manage, but it seems that it's the only way she knows, or rather it is clear I've no idea of how the rich and powerful avoid the propagation of their kind and yet appear to get enjoyment, as if the whole thing's like a glass of wine you're told is pricey though it seems the usual thin and acid stuff you drink until you're sick. And when she's gone through tactics that bemuse me, a kind of exercise that's carried out with skill and extended practice but is, after all, just training, though for what I'm quite unsure, she says, 'Well, Mr Peace, I see the name is not misplaced. At least I've done my bit for your most worthy enterprise,' and I think, 'well, yes, I suppose so, she didn't spare herself, but no impression has been left.'

I say, 'Thank you very much,' at least to be polite is easy, and I don't add 'your majesty' or 'madame', although it seems to me the kind of service that madames might give, if some girl didn't show, or didn't want.

Welcome Home

WHY, AFTER ALL, should Popov like me? If he'd left me to dangle in the crevasse, starve, perhaps, or fill with blood head down, like a fruit, it wouldn't mean that he disliked me. One kind of indifference is much like another. But he does sneer, when he says, 'While you're suspending war, why not abolish money and power – they also play a part. And history, and dignity, territory and greed, self-defence and justice, lies, sex, and beauty – that should end the Trojan war.'

I say, 'The Trojan war was resolved in a speakeasy, probably called The Horse. The Greeks went in their downtime, drank a little with the Trojan pacifists, and dreamed up the idea of a wooden horse. Full of soldiers. Yeah, of course! Trundling in the main gate. Who could doubt it. Look, a present!' But he's not intrigued.

'Go with it Stag, instead. The glory. The sacrality. What made us Russians sprawl across those goddam steppes, and down where we embraced the people who don't like us, believing, speaking, all kinds of wayward things that neither we nor you could understand. Look at your cheek! Who'd fight a battle to get one of those?' He laughs. 'And so we found another set of obstacles, of destinies to combat – don't like empire? Right, try socialism instead. Who'd you prefer, us or our enemies? And so on. And now – see what liberation means? War, Stag. Money, arms. No, Stag, stop climbing that wall of mirrors, hold your nose, accept, the only thing that's fine that comes from walking on this earth is magnificence, the dream, the word of God, driving destiny, the licence of the chief – who breaks the rules, who lets you break them too, become a bit like him, to hell with all the others, to hell with you as well.'

Maybe if Skullface heard him he'd object, 'The Institute must take all sides, we seek the truth, not transcendental victories.'

And Popov laughs again, a nasty laugh. 'It doesn't matter what the Boss's motives are. Instead, you must ride forth, in front. On your horse there's only one way you can face.'

He lightens up. 'At least the shoe problem is resolved for now.'

I comfort him: 'You've still got a stub left.'

'It should get me a promotion. My mother always wanted me to make colonel.'

I say, 'The rest of us is stuck at major. And we should've had combat boots.'

'Not with our rank. We get observer sneakers, but no boots.'

*

Skullface thinks the mission quite a triumph.

'The chiefs will love it that we've got a casualty, and only lost a foot. But your guys are getting slack – you shouldn't let them play that tape – maybe I'll send in the complete Varèse – that'll show them all! And not a word, young Stag, about your sufferings. Everyone around you is suffering much worse, at least you've had your spot, met a few presidents, their wives – the dumpy ones from east, and in the west, you see they've got the class – nude models, starlets, actresses, and a few with boyfriends. Century of the uncommon man, end of the dull, the privileged few.'

I wonder where he stands, old Skullface, not a minority representative, but yet – his squadrons of monkeys, aliens – and alas, my Anna – he's not the chief you might expect.

And I think that some of the guys here have doctorates in economics, although they can't be keeping up with news and views, and maybe Skullface should discriminate a little more, make some distinction between us autonomists and the Mild Boys, Wild Boys.

'We're all behind you, Stag,' he says. 'We don't want these guys to have their way, but compromise – that may mean precious nought – is what we try to sell. As well, of course, as guns and okra, and keeping sweet our friends over the ridge, the ones that's following your music. Have them keep it down, Stag, you don't know who'll come and see, and then there'll be the bombs, and some more hundreds, maybe thousands, prospectors with their rifles – most deplorable, on all sides, upsetting families, clans, and then, my God, you'll have the preachers and the editorialists in! Historians and their brooms, to stack you and your detritus into heaps – heaps of "I told you so", if only you'd been listening.'

And I think, 'What does he want of us, this old devil?' and I dream of Anna.

*

I say to my successor, 'Must we go on calling you John Doe?' though that is really what distinguishes him, and that alone.

'Till we get a task that needs another name,' he says, 'And incidentally, who are these funny little fellows the boss talks about? Not Iranians?'

'No,' I say, 'It's the stuff in the computers that criticises him, or else screws up the system.'

John Doe says, 'Hah, Iranians. They hanged people from tall cranes. Takes a real civilisation to do that.'

I almost envy him the calculations he'll have to make – maybe the parts of atom bombs, carried cautiously along the ancient roads. Or maybe their day too is done.

He says, 'Of course you can have faith and not pray. And pray a lot because you don't believe in anything,' and I agree: 'Tiles falling from the roof.'

And he adds, 'Yes, or rogue monkeys,' and I sense that beneath his well-tuned flab there beats a dissident heart. We think of Harry Snadders and his fall.

*

Afasian writes in a storm of reproof, 'Hey, you guys! Think strategy! Think politics! Think specifics! Culture days are over – you said ideology was finished, then you re-invent it, call it peace, stability, what you will – those days are gone. Back to the beginning! And you can forget the rumour that I wanted votes for animals. Yes, it's true it's one way of seeing that you've rights – but the logistics, guys! Arks all over – and the goats won't vote for sheep, and you can imagine foxes getting chicken votes...'

Old Skullface is amused, for after all, his scams are only that, and one campaign's as good as any other when it's failed, though even better when it wins.

And Beest joins in, it seems to me that they communicate. Maybe I'm stupid, like friends when one leads the other on for years and at one blow the game is up, account is settled, tears and bankruptcy, all that stuff and recriminations and hurt pride. So better then, on with the next, and Mr Beest insists, 'My rocks will see you through – stones into bread, my Personal Cards will make a fortune,' but I fear that now the wind has changed, we're clinging to what little secret selves we have, and even telling lies about us isn't funny any more, but he's alert, he knows the stones are in Apollo's fief, and we're the link.

Old Skullface says, 'To break those rocks you need another macho guy like our Stag here to do the deal, and at the moment I'm right out,' and of course, poor Popov's lame and Anna's wanted for her duties down in the motel, and Cai's too full of acid to take on running through the forest like a bambi – and I fear that as celebrity, ex, my price is high, and anyway, I'm through, the exercise is over, and I think, 'I don't give a shit for peace or war, it isn't in my province,' and I'd like to stay with Petra, maybe sharing a kebab, give her something good to have her bite instead of me, to hell with all these guys in uniform and protocol and monkeys up to trickiness – and back to maniacs and ordinary human hatreds ... But all this I don't say aloud, and now there's other operatives all clustered round, to be fresh volunteers, or try to hide, and Skullface says he's got to think, I hear him calling the motel, and here comes Anna, eyes all sharpened though the face is glum, or maybe that's my mind.

*

I hear Skullface, describing my job to my successor. 'Yes, Stag was very good at sums. This is the trick: you have the number of horses, yaks and pickup trucks: the bills of lading, insurances, the visas used and not: the bank accounts of the police, records of house buying, gambling, children: tires and string: people found and missing, arrests and bribes. A mass of things. And so you make a total, then another total – of all the missing things. The difference is all the illegal stuff that's moving. You can add arms and documents, capital and gas – it's what we call traffic analysis.'

Doe looks bemused, and says, 'I always thought spying was a dirty game – but now it sounds like banking.'

Skullface beams. 'It's just like prostitution – once a thing you struggled to avoid, the dregs and dirt of poverty, it was. But now, you talk of choice, not destiny or luck – all jobs are dodgy and precarious, you choose to have a life fragmented, one bit won't tell about another. So, spying in the morning, robbing in the afternoon, and in the evening – relaxing with some other pimps.'

*

I see Popov stick a garish picture on his desk. It is Saint Antony. I say, 'You like birds, then?'

'No,' he says. 'For my foot. St Antony stuck one on again.'

I say, 'Sure you've got the right St A., there were at least a couple?' and he winces.

*

Ah yes! The hardships: starting with flatulence and blisters, allergy to okra, gunshot and knife wounds, chemicals, losing at cards, joshing with the general, carrying heavy and explosive stuff, insomnia and sleeping sickness, bugs in the ear, politics and nothing alcoholic. Lots of running, fear of death and sadness of living, anger and silence, aggressiveness and obedience – you must experience everything in life and death, but with a will – nothing fantastic or too extrovert.

I ask my successor, 'What should I call you?'

'I'll tell you when we decide. Great work with the tea there, Stag.'

I laugh. 'But then there's the violence.'

'Not the worst thing,' he says.

'What is?'

'Who knows? Invisibility, perhaps.'

I say, 'That's true, since everyone goes ape to be seen. Remember, though, 'to thine own self be true' – and that's a mountain of things, no talk of visibility. A funny kind of truth, for sure.'

He laughs. 'You're a romantic, Stag. Surely you don't believe a day of peace resolves anything – it's just a stunt.'

'I just go along. Maybe I'm stunted too.'

He says, 'And the boss has this thing about aliens ...'

'Just a hypothesis,' I say, not convinced.

'Anyway,' he says, 'Funny guy. Great vision,' and my vision is of him and Anna.

*

A monkey appears at the window, loses its grip. We watch as it saves itself, hooks on to a wire far below, drops into the street and skitters off.

I say, 'I hope they don't think this ship's sinking,' and my successor replies, 'The boss puts everything on automatic. Maybe they're bored, the monkeys.'

A pause. He says, 'Maybe for the time being you could keep on calling me John Doe.'

I think of my name and say, 'That's a joke that's not a fraction funny, and besides you're not the first ...'

And as John Doe does his sums, he comes to see, as I did in my time, the caravans, the thoughtless yaks, bearing the makings of atom bombs, over the passes, skirting the glaciers, over the icy water, down to the plains where there are goats and geese, the rotting bodies of Toyotas, the infinite song of drivers on the caravans – seeking a sheltered place, circle of bushes or of stones, to make a little fire and pass the night.

Cai says, '"One day", they'll call you "one day man",' and laughs. 'That Anna's really quite banal, sure you must think so, Stag,' and I don't tell her that I find her too quite banal, but nicely so, or rather like us all, simplistic.

She laughs again, and says, 'That Lady business – you were mounting her as if she were a camel,' and I exclaim, 'The security tape! But that's just part of being a celebrity,' and she proceeds as if it's something that has weighed on her, 'Part, it's all part of something much more intricate – not just a plan, a stop to what you call "war" and start to something else you think that you desire. Even religion isn't all heaven or all hell.' I say:

'When we, when Skullface, had the plan of changing everything just for a day, it wasn't anything so intricate,' but I know even that, the day, was not so simple, and I think of Afasian, when he said, 'Apollo in the story was a vindictive animal – now, the one you deal with, Stag, do you think he's waiting for a day of rest? Is that the scheme – or something else?'

And Cai is always wrestling with that 'something

else', the step behind the step that Skullface takes, and being king is not just ordering executions, and Mr Beest insists,

'Resources you can't eat or drink you can at least make money with, and who knows what those stones can do, or if there's something under them, or what the hell, there's corporations and an asphalt company waiting near the ridge that hides your guys when they're challenging the powers that kill, the powers that negotiate – and send them food and bullets.'

*

A message comes from Apollo: 'I'm getting offers for the stones – tell me if Beest's reliable.'

'Apollo, they're only stones.' I say. 'Take what you can get.'

'Disasters everywhere,' he goes on. 'Rama is captured and will suffer terribly, they want to know his secrets and he hasn't any. And Hector was wounded, probably another animal, but we had to leave him, and he'll go to rehab and renounce us. Start up a bicycle shop, I shouldn't wonder,' and I think, 'Where next, the shape-shifting and the poetry, the sun, always more or less on time, usually managing to shine, light of our lives, that African sun invincible – although it's better to say "unconquered", since we don't know how things turn out,' and Apollo writes,

'I think I have to make a gesture, show that we mean business, since that's what we're going into,' and I show this to old Skullface and he pockets the note, and says,

'Mustn't be complicitous, and show we know ...' and I think of some great bang or whoosh and all the experts and the ambulances, pics in papers, the TV all marching in – and oh dear, it seems as sad as lying down and getting up. How it has changed, there in the forest, once where Bakunin's tongue gave inspiration and a challenge, now is just scuffling in the scrub and shooting at tin cans!

*

Cai says, 'Stag, if the boss is clumsy, makes too many errors, you could take over, need a celebrity to run the show.'

'Cai,' I say, 'too many projects that are finishing – the sacred texts, the junkies in the basement, who needs them, and probabilities are in a way our certainties, we've gone from monkeys hypothesising to "everything is up for trial",' but really I mean I have no project, neither deal nor vision – and Anna being neither, all there seems to wait for's Popov rising to command, and then we're finished as he has a Power behind him, which old Skullface never had, being himself both power and weakness, kicking our history along, in front, seeing where it led us.

I say to Skullface, 'There seem too many deaths around us,' but he seems distracted. He says, 'Acrobats, rather – that woman, in a sense my predecessor, swinging from the stars, all that symbolist stuff – I feel it myself, in my bones. Gotta get outa here!' he jazzes, and again I see the attraction he has for Anna.

'Lovely girl,' he says, 'But a bit dull when she's not into escaping,' and I think how we've been upstaged by that other woman with the scheme of weeks, or even months, of peace, and the whole thing seems quite tawdry.

'We found too many who say yes and then do no,' I say, but he's not bothered.

'Way of the world, dear Stag,' he says. 'You must pick up the small change if the notes pass elsewhere,' and I think of his profits from the stones, the deals with Apollo.

I tell him, and I shouldn't, about my hopes for Cai.

'You may see her as the Other, exotic and distant,' he says, 'but we don't need guys like that – and besides, she's really quite an ordinary, furious subject,' and I know that Skullface has a common touch, a talent too for training, both of us and all those monkeys, maybe the toxics and the mathematicians too – a viewing of the outlands as provinces of his own, his unexotic, life.

*

I hear Popov conspiring with my successor, Doe. He says, 'You see, with my foot, or rather the foot that you don't see, I've got to be a counsellor, not an agent. So, my idea is this, after the nonsense with young Stag, day upstaged by week and all that stuff, the videotaping of his fumble with the Lady – all for security, of course, – and then the massacre, Apollo – and the bushes, you'll have seen all that – well, I've some ideas to send us forward. All the battles will go on, whether we put our feet in or we don't. And I know all about feet put in or not. My interest is Islam. All the big brains say – to separate religion and politics, then we'll deal with them, one way or another. But think, John Doe – the old communist parties, like in France, said go and vote, reform or revolution: maybe you'll get one, maybe the other, or perhaps both. And in a generation they were dead. So, that's the strategy to follow ...'

And my successor says, 'It's not the strategy they want in Islam.'

Popov thinks a bit. 'Well, separation's what they get – imagine! politics and faith together, make us live the good life, all like kittens in a basket!' and he snorts. 'I know all about the faithful, lived with them. If you believe your faith's the truth, then more fool you, but keep it in a box away from politics, or you'll lose – even your illusions. I've been there, young Doe.'

*

Popov is frustrated, and he asks Doe about the job. Doe says, 'Stag used to count, I don't know how. It's something that for me is senseless,' and Popov says,

'As far as I saw, he called his tea dealers on the phone and asked them what the traffic was – in tea, in drugs, in arms, in people.'

'Then somewhere there's a list? Maybe the boss has made one too, for his successor, when this Harry Snadders stuff has seen him forced to go.'

Offhandedly, Popov says, 'Well, maybe Cai has got the list. Cai, or Chai.'

Doe says, 'I don't think the boss will go because he's guilty. Got fed up, more like,' and I think, 'if he goes, maybe there's Anna taking over, then maybe Cai will disappear. And the scheme for Islam is absurd, creating enemies and fighting for a generation – it's nothing that concerns me. My caravans move on and through, as they did when they could only ride the little horses, not use them for pulling weights, the people were of all clans, all faiths, and now old Skullface's fixated on Iranians, and

Popov doesn't know the way to marshal monkeys – and I feel my Petra's teethmarks. She bit deep, and goes on biting, and I don't know why, is it a cure, prevention, or just a mark, a pictogram, to show that she possesses – what? Me? It seems too small a thing.'

I think of how I couldn't tell the ministers from the drug dealers, and found myself offering a price, a quantity and quality. Arms dealers, on the other hand, were quite unmistakeable – cheery in between, loved by all sides. With jokes and catalogues.

*

Cai says, 'First, the problem was barbarism – people came from aggressive cultures, shattered the rest. It was on the marches, the borderlands, that the powerful, the outsiders, exercised all their savagery. Then it was socialism, was it the values, or the practices? And now it's Islam, but you'll see, it's passing, if it hasn't passed. What's surpassed is gone, is dying, faded. It incorporates itself. And then the wave returns. Maybe this time, more savage.'

*

Anna sidles up to me. How beautiful, how desirable, she is. Soft to look at, hard when she rescues you, soft of feature, but a man's best friend.

She says, 'Stag, my moments of intimacy with you have no equal, you know?'

I say, 'Intimacy has been quite rare, and hurried,' and she says, 'Not physical, idiot, I mean to chat, to pass the time.'

I ponder this. She says, 'I need to get cut in on those terrorists' stones. Guerrillas, terrorists, what you want to call them – they're moving out of fashion – but stones are always useful' and I tell her, 'I know all about them, where they are,' and she says, 'So does Skullface – not to be underrated, Stag.'

I think I speak of love, or at least affection, some sort of partnership, when in the evenings I finish with the phone calls – most of my guys work nights, and those with yaks or reindeer are in another time zone, but she interrupts,

'Stag! You're a former celebrity – what is there left for you to do? You've done it, done your life, all your potential mined, promoted. Forget the phone calls, John Doe will find the atom bombs, not you.'

I mention some kind of teaming up, although I know that her time out with Skullface is a problem, but Skull-face too will pass, but she is clear, she says, 'Stag, drop that old love and cling-together stuff – that's what people do who have no future, no ambition – it's for failures, not adrenalin, but some kind of valium, turns into slack euph-oria – not for me. If you feel it, Stag, just go and do it, don't romanticise. And it will pass.'

I say, 'So I'm no use to you? That may be mutual, you know,' and she says, 'I hope it is. Take a step back, you'll see it's all ridiculous. Think of the President and Lady – they're still aiming high, they have the instinct, Stag. Don't sit and mope and give things up.'

She's right, it shows indeed we can be intimate, though other states are quite as satisfying, like Petra's bite that comes to mind at various moments, and did not result from intimacy, nor anything like.

'Intimacy,' she says, 'Is the best, Stag. It lasts a

minute, or a day. It shows us we're not monkeys,' and I think, 'I'm not so sure about the monkeys. Some of them are quite attached.'

*

Anna discusses the succession. 'You, Stag, the trouble is you're famous, not a pro. And Popov, he's a Russian,' and I joke, 'Footloose, but not fancy free,' and she plods grimly on: 'You climbed a mountain, had adventures – but you've got this problem, mountains, clans, adventures – and terrorism, fame – above all, your peering through some modest person, seeing a whole historical scene – that's all imagination, all you, your head,' and I agree,

'I've nothing but my fame, it's true. Fame and my shoes. But why should Skullface leave us?' and she says, 'Take the two f's, the funny fellows – and those apes.'

'That's what makes him charming,' I say, 'those are his miracles, charisma,' and I think, 'What's happened in those lunch breaks, how can she so easily unseat her lover?' and I remember that love is an also-ran for her.

I say, 'Well then – not me, not Popov – why not Cai? All sweetness, a minority rep,' and Anna continues, 'And full of hate and ignorant of what the Institute can do,' and I react, 'This piddling Institute – what do you think it can?'

Anna's impatient, 'Don't you understand, if Skullface loses credibility, what's to become of us? We're in the loop, the network of diplomacy – we're the high priests of peace, no one can spit in our clear and optimistic eyes. We have to be attended to. We've loved the high, we stumbled steplocked with the lowly – and yet our paws–' she stops and retreats, 'Our hands are clean. Our eyes are clear.'

And then I think, so Anna has her plan, not for what to do, but how to reach the top. And that too's fine for me, because I have my fame, the less I do, the less it can be taken from me, it's like a jewel that slowly fades, safe in its box.

And so we bicker on, we're quite reactionary, I maybe most of all. I think of how the Ramayana tells us, when the pair of lovers reach their destination, the monkeys wave to them and female monkeys look out of the windows of the golden upper storey of the palace – how different from my Rama, and our monkeys in the brownstone!

*

For once, Skullface seems bothered.

'This one day peace rap,' he says, 'you know, it's a nonsense that makes sense. What sense it has, it shows that Popov's call to history, riding a white horse, follow my leader, grannie's footsteps and the glory of old Muscovy – is all a tawdry makeshift. It's just a pretty blanket. And now we've got to handle the girl that wants peace for a week, and then there'll be the sportsman bidding up – a month! And someone, maybe some tall poppy, president of what, will up us to a year. Stag, imagine the anticlimax of a week! How difficult to sidle round a month of pause in all those shipments, exercises, raids – the training alone, and think of all the infiltrations, the spooks will run like spiders, everyone will sneak in here and buy up that. A year – my dear boy – just think, what a bagarre!

'A day, now, that's the not-too-long that makes you

think of wanting something more, but not exactly what, you understand. That is the trick – you see it coming, then it's gone, nothing has changed, but maybe, maybe ... and you, dear Stag, retain your status. He who made it happen! What? you will ask – and so, it's no one's job to give the answer. No one asks the guys who promised to end poverty – "After your failure, what comes next?" For we all know, the answer's "Just another campaign to make whatever it may be – happen." We must be macho about it.

'Maybe you could fuck the opposition, the "week-peace" girl, cut a deal, who knows, a marriage somewhere, or a birth?'

I say, 'I think her backers have all that worked out – her future's planned, and anyway – the peace guys rutting in some luxury suite – it moves attention from what is, or is not, the point,' and sadly he agrees.

*

Cai says, 'I don't romanticise you, you know,' and I reply, 'Maybe I romanticise – I see you as the weak subject, weak in history.' If her bosses want her back, she's precarious, like the institute. I fear for her. I try to shut out cement and skyscrapers, railroads, oil wells, all the trash that overlays my yaks and caravans and camels.

'Perhaps you'll find stones, like Apollo, make a killing ...' I say, and pause, remembering the warning Skullface pocketed, and how the threads must never be neglected lest the pattern's lost, and Cai explains, 'We're full of valuable stones and stuff, we even wish we didn't have so much, return to live in song and legend, as they say, the tourists say,' and quickly I tell her, 'You still hunt with royal eagles, and yet, your real life's full of despots, poverty, all that ... I tell you, I've no vision. I see all sides and yet am blind. I don't even believe in Skullface and his funny little fellows, and God knows, it should be easy to believe in what's invisible.'

And I know my time with Cai is up, for she's off somewhere, clattering of invisible hooves.

*

Skullface expresses concern about Apollo and the massacres. 'In and out,' he says, 'Our operation without moral responsibilities. Nor, we proposed, political ones.'

We have a bioethics committee, part of our life insurance. Bioethics: 'There's a laugh', says Anna.

We have a session about the monkeys. Now I'm a celebrity, and whatever happens if that status dies or lingers, the monkeys have taken to carrying little cameras, snapping us all, through the windows. I guess they sell the prints. But we mostly talk about the ficus each office has – it's standard issue, it's a rebarbative plant, ungiving and delicate, and some would like them dead – no problem with their propagation, as we're told their roots are boiled, but they cling to being moribund, quite tenacious.

Old Skullface has converted the monkeys' typing to simple secular texts; he says the basement's stuffed with too much divinity, there's no one gets to make a choice, the old tongues and alphabets are generating experts but no faith.

He says down there the monkeys have a thing about the ficus, maybe some latent memory, there is a vast dark hall, they've collected all they can, and there the ficus die and rot, the monkeys not seeing that they must give light and water.

This new, transitional, regime has meant Cai's ancient book is nearly ready, a New Age edition, due to become a selling miracle, now it's 'only connect', so everything is part of everything else, and Cai says that it may be true but rather dull, and where does she fit into this? And Skullface tells her she must be a sport and team is all, and planning projects better fun than realising them, and I think of Anna, wonder what his project can be there, but anyway, I see that Anna's depths, if such there are, are depths for her and not for me.

Cai says, 'You're very delicate with us minorities, Stag, but we fought hard to keep our space, when 'they' came riding through. All of them.'

'Well,' I say, 'At least you gave them – some of them – an alphabet. Something they'd never had.'

'So what?' she says.

'With alphabets you can cut deals, write contracts, unless you're too busy riding your horse, driving your Toyota,' and she looks at me like I'm a piece of rock.

Skullface organises a memorial ceremony, for the villagers killed. We stand out in the courtyard. He's hired three trumpeters. They are very tall. They strike some screaming heights, their silver instruments are making icicles, it's cold as hell, and they go screeching up and down, the bored and friendly faces take a glaze of ice, the leaves fall off the trees. The tallest trumpeter goes higher, goes highest up the mountain, only he above the clouds, to seek out that last soldier, clump of comrades, freezes, casts them down. Into the glacier. This is death. And memory preserved.

*

And I think, old Skullface, what a bastard, but a clever bastard too. Anna says, ‘We should have our little telephones sound off together, as if the dead are calling us,’ and someone tells her hush, for once she does. Poor Popov is having trouble with his standing, and I see he has a shoe on his good foot that’s far above his status, but of course he only need buy one shoe – I wonder what he does with the unneeded one, maybe he’s got a friend that’s lost the other foot, they met in hospital, go to the store together. And Anna’s wearing little slippers, silver sequins all over, Cai has knitted boots, and I must wear these goddam sneakers, for as I’m still celebrity, the sneakers are the way I’m recognised.

The monkeys swarm up from their room, correcting the bibles having been suspended. They form fours, I think no one has formed fours for decades – they’ve five fingers, so in fives is natural, but fours needs training and I guess that Skullface has been down drilling them, something he couldn’t do with toxics, who don’t show, it being bad taste to have them celebrate the dead, them in communion with death and every non-living thing and state.

All the best heroes do a deal with monkeys, they make good troops, and keep their word, but how they suffer, and I think on freely, leaping from banal thought to the sublime and back again, and Skullface takes the monkeys down to tea and biscuits and we’d go too, but trumpet music goes on until the climax, when we’re all at last all frozen in our tombs, surrounded by our useless jewels and bits of food and sacrifices. I wish I’d never gone with the guerrillas, seems you can’t have mourning without complicity.

And then the snappers come, of course I'm still the celebrity, they take me from all sides, although the world's forgotten if we had our day of peace or not, I'm still the peg they hang existence on.

Expressionless, I give them all my image, so they can remember and work through some emotion, though I'm sure they don't remember if I'm a hero or a baseball star, and in the end who cares, it's all in history now, and so I set my face in silent sorrow. And at last it's done, and we are all alive, and go to have our drinks.

*

One last throw of the dice, is what Skullface proposes. I fly to see Apollo. He's now minister for Rec and Tech – reconciliation and sun services – also, the hunt for aliens in computer systems.

'You're quite the statesman now,' I say.

'I always was, it's just I don't do shapeshifting any more.'

We chat about Hector, Rama, both physically mashed up but mentally in rehab. 'And Bakunin?' I ask. He seems abstracted: 'Stag, you never even wanted the clock turned back or forward, just wanted the end of clocks. You should learn when to turn the other cheek, haha,' and tries to embarrass me, a gesture at my cheek.

'We'll see your mountain, El'brus, version green!' he laughs. 'The caravans disarmed, just migrants seeking work and honest toil – with benefits, and all that stuff, of course.'

Old Skullface wants a bargaining, perhaps he'd settle for a month of what he still calls peace, Apollo says they're waiting for a ship, and till it docks I can have what Skullface wants, but talk of arms and ships and months is not my interest, so I say,

'If all else fails, young Anna'll take the boss's place,' and so Apollo laughs,

'A feisty gal, I heard you two attaining your paradise – a way off, in the bushes,' and I can object, but don't, and then he says, 'You may be worth a final whirl, young Stag, just for old times,' and I think that maybe I'm to lose a foot, or just another bite, or maybe meet with Petra, and I sense Afasian throwing up his hands – he's living with his Hindu lady now, gives up his politics, been converted to a pragmatism that mostly leaves him speechless, while Mr Beest, if it is he and not a partnership and bank, has settled down here, mining stones. I don't want to see them, either of them, willowy voices on the air, and so Apollo says again, 'One last adventure, Stag, you must be game,' but game or not, play or the hunt, I don't have a choice, and off we go.

'I cut out all this nonsense,' says Apollo, pointing to the motorcycle escorts as our motorcade moves off, 'Except for security, of course,' and he hands me a bag of Beest Corp sweets, throwing from his own bag to the children running alongside. In the distance we see a hump rising from the scrubby ground. I see some of the older kids have tattoos like my cheekmarks, and Apollo says, 'We tried to do you proud, you being a celebrity, role model too, for all that climbing, rescuing, deep philosophising too,' and I see the hump is a Mount El'brus, green indeed, reduced in size and snow- and ice-less. On the lower slopes some scavenging is going on, and up above, where the glacier might have started, kids throw each other down, and then scale up again.

'We thought of calling it Mount Stag,' he says, 'but since there's lots of countries' cash went to it, we felt a flexible name, changing when each delegation comes, would be in order.' Then he apologises, 'I couldn't fore-warn the snappers, but they caught you at the airport,' and in any case I'm used to them, and if they're not around I think I must be in the wrong town, so what the hell, and poor Mount Stag is rather feeble.

'This isn't much of an adventure,' I say.

He laughs, 'Just wait and see.'

And I think 'Oh no, not Petra,' as it's clear he knows my story and my history, and so I wait, and dread.

We pass the Pax Eterna cemetery, where the dogs seek bones, the little stalls that sell Stag shoes – we reach the lower slopes, I think of it as Mount Reform, and Apollo's pleased:

'My motto is "every day anew" – the more you ann-ounce the changes, greater is the change,' and we climb round the hummock's side and see a hall, tin roof, with thugs outside, and no doubt inside too. Apollo says, 'I'll leave you here, my story takes another twist – and so does yours.'

And here is Petra, but she can't be here, can't be the Petra that bit me. I have all the pieces, but not the message.

Cai's book, had a fine, comprehensive message, or at least a story, but it no longer holds. Those nomads are long dead, and before they died they mixed in with the rest of us, made us ascetics and hedonists, believers and agnostics, made us Skullface's Iranians. The message holds its shape, but doesn't tell. Or else it's just a story.

Beest makes money, Afasian has found a rich woman and renounced politics, Anna runs the show. Beest is making money from the stones. He can make his money when we've all lost ours and have to search for something in us that is entertaining, can be sold.

And entertainment's here! In this loud hall, the tin roof booms, we're all dancing, screaming, singing, and my bitten cheek burns with its signs, as if they're the first strokes and points of what will be an alphabet. It seems – it is – the President without his Lady! He's trying to get up, he tries to make it out, but there is such a press, a press of bodyguards and spooks and snappers, that he falls, is thrust down, doesn't rise. I'm dancing and I'm screaming along with Petra, like the rest, and we are all good mates, although the languages are not the same or even similar, and the songs may have a rhythm, but all overlayed, and each one beats whatever he can find, a fist, a foot, a head, a chair, trying to assert, and with a happy face. We are enjoying ourselves! And I see Apollo peeping through the doors, he'll break this up, he'll show himself, and we'll be going, leaving to go on about our normal day, shop or beg or hammer tin.

But no, it doesn't end, there's jostling, and I'm still inside. Petra, or her twin, looks critically at me, I say, 'No more biting,' and she says, 'No, it's quite distinctive as it is, another one would give it symmetry, too much.'

All the guys are doing what their customs let them do, to enjoy themselves – too much perhaps – the drinkers drink, and I see Georgian brandy, the sniffers sniff, some others do religion, others abstain but sing and stare like hawks – everyone is singing, trying to dance. And women are around, pouring out booze, or picking up the fallen men, or showing off or getting drunk or being hit or who knows what, and we are all a load of monkeys, living on our wits, but maybe not so clever as the apes, though each group has its culture and I think, 'Stopping those drugs is like stopping snow melting in the spring' and where I once saw caravans, now I see Toyotas, migrants, and tourists, the whole world singeing itself a little, just the edges, and here the guys are having so much fun, and Security is getting loud, and they've got guns, and so a space is made around them.

And Petra sees me drift away, and says, 'You've always done your best,' and I think, 'Worse than that you cannot say,' and do I dream, or is that another president, from the Americas this time, brought in to see us having fun, and there's Apollo, ushering in, and making his excuse to leave us simmering here. And Petra says, 'You'd better try your pitch – this guy looks smart, at least as these things go,' and here he is and asks me what I've got, peace or drugs.

'Nothing but my fame,' I say.

He's puzzled and I guess fame is what he breathes, and I don't feel he's open for a few days' peace, him steering by the stars and casual omens, no doubt large sacrifices, done by a pontifex, animals burnt and maybe people too, and so I'm quiet, and maybe that's a novelty, I turn away, and he must think he's gone invisible.

But fantastic is the noise, the dancing, now the shooting off – maybe it's fireworks, but it isn't likely – and I'm with Petra on the floor, and how I wish that I am back with the monkeys inventing bibles and the Word of God, and even Skullface off to the motel, and surely I have won my day, or even two, of peace, but no. No.

Petra is here.

I know we shall all suffer for the trampling of the President.

Still, I shall live on with my fame till it expires. And

as for Cai, I think she lives not by the book, but by the fire that burnt its author – an anger I can't match, but maybe should. And the scars that Petra leaves will heal, not disappear – the first strokes of an alphabet, perhaps.

If that's what they call hope, it's rather slight, but if you hope for stupid things, then you'll be lost – the real point is to leave this room, the guys are singing till they burst, it's marvellous, it's horrible – and here's Apollo, sliding down the hill, he presses in my hand – a book of poems, ministerial stamp. It's fame for him, a fame on fame, he lives it day to splendid day, I don't begrudge him, how in any case to judge a person who's acquired charisma and a motorcade? The little boys – I notice that the girls are still indoors – run up to beg and steal a little of his light. Blessed are they all, I think, as I walk to my aeroplane, and leave my Petra far behind, her mystery, I am pleased to say, has not yet been revealed.

Conclusion

CAI ALMOST TENDERLY looks at my teethmarks, she says, 'It could be the pictogram for two flutes. If it had been me, I'd leave something more definite behind for you – a watch-tower, perhaps,' and I think, ah, dear Cai, resentments so well buried, no room for me. She's off again, while masses start their big adventure – making a new America in the east – she's just an egg in someone else's omelette. Yet she's a spy, has made it to the viewing platform, price is compromise, but then, she's feet in both the stirrups, more than you can say of Popov! His Revolution cancelled out, not just transformed! So farewell Cai – dragging the others, being dragged, into our world, our Institute. And still there's Anna ...

Suddenly we hear what seems a trumpet call. A shriek, defiant, summoning. We look outside, see nothing, then the word spreads – monkeys on the roof! We run outside – there's like a rampart high above, crammed with defiant creatures, their teeth shine out like cabuchons, they scream, they wave. Although in all the stories and the pictures they're excellent with bows, here we don't keep bows and arrows for the animals, so these weapons, lances, must be our aerials and satellite junk and all the stuff that's kept up there, even the poles for laundry, how should I know.

And then there's Skullface – his great skull makes him look like Doctor Death, he shouts to me, 'You must assert – that I had absolutely nothing to do with planting you with that Apollo, vindictive brute he is, and capable of anything, as maybe we all are, and covering up and justifying. Nothing to do with planting you, and so I had to have you rescued, and that cost poor Popov's foot, but then our Anna brought it off, it had to be authentic, or we'd have lost the peace!'

So lost it anyway, I thought, and Cai says, 'War – real spies, real revolutionaries must accept it as part of their business,' and Anna says with pleasure, 'War is part of everyone's business.' I think of Apollo's mission, Bakunin's revolution through the unions, that dusty syndicalism, was heresy to everyone, to Marx and all the governments, the army of disorganised, and not to speak of union bosses, and indeed, it is, has always been, of all lost causes the most lost. Then there's Popov, with John Doe, who knows no better – but he has to think of future prospects even if they kill him – so they make a pair and stand for honest peace, against old Skullface and manipulation. I know that Popov's not like that at all, but he plays destiny, combined with planning and the well-schemed stab – and certainly old Skullface is losing parts, since he's had to call out the monkeys.

Anna says, 'Monkeys are simply loyal, so in that way they're independent, they depend only on one person, they're pledged to him, the one and supreme boss.' And I think, the monkeys were around in ancient times, that's how they write the books of God and gods because they write their memoirs, garden of Eden. Monkey Adam. Monkey Eve. Quite innocent. In time, shapeshifting into human form. Animal clan especially favoured, taking part in battles when the humans were too few to risk, I see them driving chariots, mounds of sacrificed bananas, no doubt the typewriter their special instrument, keeping up the link with creator and creation – now, for the moment, slowed right down, confined to machines and messages

... no monkey prophecies, the battles lost, the armour twisted, holed and junked. And as I muse, I hear old Skullface shout, 'Don't let the toxics up,' but they are safe behind their door, so too the families of Probability – they won't come up to join the battle, on this or other side. I picture them smoking their meerschaums, though I only ever saw their printouts. Then there is a clamour – a handsome monkey loses grip, or else is pushed.

Moment of fear and dread. He lies there, broken on the ground, and Anna says, 'Poor little bugger,' a soldier's lament indeed. And Cai says, 'Fear and dread. Poor innocent' and I think, 'Or maybe not, what anyway can innocence mean, what help is that, if we're popped off, being innocent's just euphemistic for "unarmed".'

Now I see that Popov, followed by John Doe, is climbing up the building. I notice the whole facade has little ladders, branches, even with small painted faces, like a snakes-and-ladders board, pointing the way, and though Popov's foot is surely missed, he makes good time, and Doe is puffing on behind, his trousers following, for I see he has an old-time military gut, that isn't made for western clothes, maybe the Greeks wore tunics when they scaled the walls, as with all that lamb and lobster they were putting on the beef, and I imagine – my – Hector, lean as a strip of ape, spearing a hundred as they try to waddle up – although the picture is more Rama's, with its air of massacre and intervention, maybe divine or mostly not.

Popov and Doe are nearly there, the monkeys on the ramparts scream, though who has an idea of what to do, I cannot think – old Skullface leads the monkeys, but they've never shown desire to kill us unless they're ordered to, and Skullface now must mind his back and also not appear to rule the show but now they're nearly at the top, our mountaineers – and no! Popov mistakes a painted ladder for a wooden one, he loses hold, he teeters there, a monkey holds a pole, maybe to help him, though it is no help, maybe to push him off, maybe another possibility – he falls, so slowly, as if he's brought a personal glacier to preserve him, his monstrous sideburns and his apple cheeks, he falls and falling, in the sky outlined, the leg, the absent foot, is fixed against the blue, the victim, traitor, loyal to himself alone. Or maybe some government will mourn him, who knows, their motives are never ours, and as he falls, John Doe puts out a hand. I think, 'Oh no, you mustn't spoil the picture, spoil the destiny,' but he is follower, bit player, obedient to some vague project that's not ours, looks only forward; not to our life's puzzles and our schemes, the books of god, the drugs so lavishly left round, the weapons, from the rocks to all the other killing tools, until we see the long distance ones, the chemicals, the bombs – and maybe worst of all, the books. Doe falls. In silence, selfless gesture unacknowledged. For a moment both are caught – a three-footed hieroglyph against the sky. I imagine in the foyer of some building a picture of the two, maybe a mosaic, sculpture even, a double Icarus, a fall of men, and then they're down, we see their faces, last few seconds, try to sum it up, the whole of life's experience, so much to tell, the images and mountains – that's for Popov – and for Doe, maybe assault courses and a questionnaire or two, equipped him for the spying trade, but not too well. For he is loyal, like the monkeys, and it doesn't do him good.

But Skullface is now desperate – that's three operatives gone, counting poor Harry Snadders in, and complicity is strong in every case. The plan for peace is shreds, career for him requires a really fine press conference to shrug off blame, reveal the plan beneath that makes the errors seem good sense or fate – or how maybe someone else was sabotaging the fine plan to save mankind, or at least to make the waiting more attractive.

The monkeys cheer and wave their spears, and Anna goes to Skullface and she says, 'We got them, chief.' There on the ground, the shattered monkey, now with two warriors on top, he didn't break their fall. Their eyes are open, but their brains have leaked, as if the beauty and the wonder are too great for single minds to apprehend, and Cai calls up the stretcher party, and we're fewer, but more noble too.

Finale

WE ARE STANDING, Anna, Cai and myself, looking through our window, and we are thankful it is bulletproof. There is a great confusion, a pattering, a wafting. I think of magnificent, fleshed-out white flowers, growing like magic beanstalks, as from below there is a frush, a nearing, a scrambling out.

We see Skullface, smiling tranquilly. He is being borne aloft by all his monkey clan – they do not seem to cling but fly. Without a sound they came down from the roof and mustered. I think I hear the cries – 'Peace', 'Equality', 'in freedom', and he is higher, higher. I think I hear the trumpets, but it may be sirens. Now the traffic stops, down below there is a roaring, maybe it is crowds, what can they make of this, event without a death or wound or cop?

And Anna says, 'OK – but equality in monkeyland is no great deal', and I think, '"Peace" – we'll see how far they carry him, what deals he has in mind, what resources to be dug,' and Cai says quietly, 'Freedom it may be, for he is free from us, the messes he has made – and in a sense he's also king, albeit of a tribe in nature. See how they love him, Stag.'

'Yes,' I say, 'but they just take orders, and independence is not the greatest gift for apes, they shake their paws with powerful guys – who they may love, and even worship,' and she says:

'I don't think that they appraised his orders, maybe the monkeys are mechanical, not pondering the consequences or the motivations. It's just wired in, not to take too serious,' and I must say I'm not convinced: there seems an awful distance between the flying wedge of monkeys, their discipline, and our jumbled standoffs in the forest or the jungle. I wonder who will write the sacred texts, now that the monkey clan has flown away. It all seems rather sad, as we disciples watch in safety from our office, as the mangod who has brought us here and given us our worthless tasks flies far away, jewel clasped in a cluster of monkey hands.

Apotheosis

AND THE NOISE below is louder, fiercer, and I hear some chants, or maybe it's for football clubs or executions, but it's clear the whole event has entered in the social, the guys with sound equipment and the satellite stuff are doing interviews – it's taking off, maybe the Boss had wished it so, it has become event, and us – celebrities! The bearers of his truth, expounder of his problems, unresolved, enduring.

THE BRIGHT STARS

Mais, maintenant, nous sommes au théâtre. Voici que le rideau se lève....

(Alain Robbe-Grillet,
Pour un nouveau roman)

IT IS A DREADFUL PLACE. I go in. It is a sooty place, a black hall. I see it hung with bats, the foam comes out of the seats, they'd be better made of wood, or concrete arcs. It's a warehouse, that we call a theatre. The musicians have a pit, a hole, yes, in one corner there is standing water. What it needs is some hero, spurring up the lighting, summoning up ushers. Now, empty, banal. Not a metaphor, just nothing; rather, something dark, it smells of boots.

The director, Igor, says, 'Gilded pills, yes they slip down – what do they heal?' But healing's not his game. On his stage there is no death, 'It trivialises,' he says. Instead there's suffering, laid on with relish. But it's all a show. What troubles me is that brash laughter coming from below, sometimes it seems beneath our feet an engine snarts and crackles, there is a pause, maybe some music like it's squeezed from stones. Then days of silence.

Igor puts on shows, he's a spectacularist. He's also my friend. My girl, Katya, acts for him, maybe she's his girl too. As actors are.

Igor instructs me, his ideas. And back there, where I'm not at home, they're starting up the killing, small-scale, vendettas, old scores become new scores – only if you slaughter the kids will you have – well, not peace but resentment seething to the cemetery. Killing is right, it comes from our experience, and though it's stupid, sure makes its point. And down we go, for justice, our good cause.

Igor says, 'I need human voices, they give warmth, a carpet of illusions, and more, always you need more, I think about sixteen, talking and singing, you don't need words, or to distinguish them, but those instruments, so limited, yet you can make them loud, so loud, they call and trill like birds. The poor things, you can make them do anything, they'll make love or kill themselves, so willing.'

I say 'Obedient,' and he, 'No, not at all, but willing, finding a plot, grasping so quickly how the tragedy ends.' I say, 'Always tragedy?' and he, 'What do you expect, immortality? When it's over for the evening, back in their box they go. And you must pull them out again, they dance upon your strings.'

And I think of those recordings, Austrians of 1944, clapping like mad at Richard Strauss, then out to meet their horrible ends, and after having killed so many. Nothing cancels out, and maybe Igor's right, these moral tales are only fables, stick in the mind but nothing more, just glue of plot. They're all there, prancing and yodelling on – inaudible until you open up the box.

And Igor says, 'It's just obsession. But no one really dies, and while you're planning it, you live!'

Drama is alien to me, an orphan by profession.

I remember – the neighbour sleeping on the cobbles

when it was hot inside his house, kept drugs in his vacuum cleaner. Another – who imported cocaine in painted plastic life-size trees, tried to kill me with a log. The basalt columns, they say there was a temple of Cybele, triangulates with Macedonia and Izmir, anywhere triangulates with anywhere else, and those black stumps are everywhere. Like burnt-out trunks – we'd no nature left, just houses, safe houses, for penitents and not – all styles and none. The white buffaloes, that disappeared from their wallow by the river – then came decorative swans, stolen to eat when there were feasts. Eaten, like the pigs they butchered in the gutter, blood like mine running down to somewhere, blond lashes and pink skin becoming white.

Neighbour who said, 'Blow on the head gives a sharper edge to reality' – concerned about my head, though those swans were killed horribly. Remembering things that don't give you an identity – Igor says that gangs can kill below the level of the media, could be an epidemic.

And my girl acts, though she can't sing – will she be acting, making love to Igor? Odd profession, throwing yourself into any passing imagination.

Igor's friend has a limousine, and Igor goes with him to collect clients, and then walks home – keeping fit in luxury.

I have a Serbian name. I administer the money that may pay for him. His shows.

I belong to a leper country, the bosses make us responsible for the history they wished to make. I have never lived there, never attached. The name's enough. My demons are alive, like children's toys, fresh in their boxes twenty years on. Every detail bright, but never played with. Dressed up a little, can't shoo them to the past –

living with injustice that can never be appealed, yet weighs like guilt. And so I feel at home in Igor's play – choices that aren't, retribution from all sides, rescue that kills.

I've my doubts about Igor and the spectacle he's planning, he's obsessed by what they were watching – in Moscow, wasn't it? – when the commando, women, widows, armed, what they hell did they want, blow it all up? 'North' something, wasn't it? I forget, everyone's forgotten. And then the special forces came in and made it all real drama, my God, – the gas, the buses full of rescued people dying, stacked like dried cods, he wants to make the drama.

My God, those poor Chechens, and the killing there, and now the Russians too – and Capital comes in, you can't destroy it – but that other capital they did, Grozny, and now all neat, rebuilt without the people, no one remembers now nor maybe cared a lot just then, he wants to make a stage that has it all: a civil war, the music, and the musical. The audience that becomes the corpses, commando struck down with all their military junk. A putrid scheme, it makes you feel clean and free just to think it, then to extract maybe another big idea – but then you throw it off like something dirty, another of the little nightmares we hope burn off at dawn.

All blown away, shot, burnt, decapitated, buried in ruins, crushed under tanks, slit open, starved or bludgeoned, then gassed, neglected, saved to be killed, revenged, forgotten. Or resurrected – those that remember, those that grieve, maybe they find that Igor's scheme, that Igor's person, is something ugly, ambiguous, is something putrid, made for himself alone, not at the level of their reality, some kind of therapy to make him feel.

Fable of suffering, as if it happened centuries ago.

To make it, on the stage, happen all over. To accomplish what? Resolve, depict, or just to shock and make some bucks?

And I can say, you'll get the cash, more likely you *might* get the cash – but you can't bring the people back, it's all gone by, another country, no one character to make you cling, sit firm. Just invented figures gripped by ideas or circumstance, action or innocence.

All over! – out you walk, no gas, no guns, no buses, a piece of history, and you think – maybe the killing's not the point, it's culture, religion, policies and plots, the practicalities, errors, soldiers think in their way, then try to think like those guerrillas, widows some, or warriors – how did they think, maybe spaced out or tricked. And who can read those clans, decide who planned it all? Not the killing, then, but the responsibility – but then, and after all, what does that do, we're sitting in our seats, thinking great thoughts at Igor's big idea (sheer vanity). What a pity.

Igor defends himself – for these are early days, and later he just runs ahead. It seems I've seen the horror and the trick, but missed the point.

'You miss the complexity, and so the reality of life – you counterpose concepts and deplore the results. I know, it's because you're Serbian – though a good liberal one. Neighbours killing neighbours – then you see they are like you, they are you, and so you say "halt". But everyone else, it's not either-or, universal us and them, death, suffering. And 'Bring us together, all.' For the rest – it's the rules. Rules of being. The rules count, you know. If you've no rule, just being cruel and seeking vengeance, so that every atrocity's part of your suicide, you do and then are done to, so you miss the essence. The tragedy. The culture. Not "what" but how and when and why.'

I say, 'Igor, I just hand out the money. I am not a Serbian. Anyway, you see emotion coming from those rules, you want that audience permanent, gassed but alive, sitting there under your spell. That's not the rules,' and Igor says, 'It's my rules, rules of my game.'

*

Do we hope, putting on this play, or finding guys who can put fingers in your brain and open up the light, that we shall reach a truth? Whether it's complex or direct, what will these corpses serve, when Igor's turned them into eloquent ghosts, the technique polished, all of life is there, the actors act – behind them, not to be seen, the lovers, agents, landlords, bankers, magi?

I worry about Igor, can he keep up with the pace of the world? And so appear contemporary? And fill the stage – all the contents he couldn't put into books, making an audience, that leaves – satisfied? He wants to make the public choose. Commando, widow, spectator, soldier – survivor or dead. Choice. Not destiny.

What choice can an audience in a theatre have? One public watching the drama of another. Like it's seen itself? Who are they, what are they, these battered brainy elves and demons? It seems to me like the White Knight – the childish play: the song, the title of the song, the plagiarism, the something else that is the song but not the song you hear. Hear? Are you supposed to hear it? That Russian musical, where everyone was gassed, the paying audience, the – maybe – paid guerrillas, terrorists, the religious, killers, trussed-up bundles of black, armed and inert. It seems to me like home, home in a fable, fairy tale, it can only be so horrible and entertaining, brainy, if you shut it in a theatre.

Well, if the world weren't full of coincidences, it wouldn't be the world. But must it also be solipsistic? Well, yes, I guess so.

I worry about Katya. I worry about myself. Can she keep up with the pace of the world, Igor's world? What would we lose if he failed to put it all in, all Northwest, whatever it was called? Some angle, some injustice, fresh uncovered, some mass grave of circumstance and fantasy. Yes, we'd lose some angle. Bring in the crowds, tickle their fancy and tweak it, tease them. He tells me,

'No, Milan – it's not like that. If I understand you, you're standing too far back. You should go into the jungle, learn to live with everything you find there, even if they eat your soul.'

I ask, 'How do you put Faust in with all those poor people, martyrs who wanted to be, martyrs who didn't know a thing, victims before and victims after?'

Igor says, 'If you're eating scrambled eggs you don't need to know about chickens.'

'The trouble is, the bosses think you're a fraud, unqualified.'

He laughs. 'If you're a creative, how do you "qualify"?'

'They say, "Read books, win prizes, have tattoos."'

'They're cretins.'

I may agree, but say, 'You're rubbish, Igor.'

'Milan, you're crap.'

I object, 'I'm supposed to be.'

*

He says, 'Do you know what happens right here, beneath your feet?' and he points at the stage decking, at the trapdoors where they used to come up from hell. 'Down there, there's the Bright Stars.'

He looks triumphant, and it will take much time before I understand.

I say, 'Just tell me what you need.'

'I will.'

'You don't mean to gas the public in their seats?'

He spits a grin, a mask somewhere between comedy and tragedy. He says, 'You liberals, with your moralising bluster – the last of you, you Americanisers, how many thousands did you manage to educate? – blast them away, and if you're too few, then suicide and bomb-blasts, off with their heads, in sacks, into the historic river,' and his hating face comes into mine. 'Your bloody crowd, you have the better rhetoric. And now the name is "all humanity". Just try saying, "Feed me, I'm hungry," and "if you don't, I've got a gun", and then you'll see how far humanity will get you.'

'So you will gas them? If I give you the money?'

He's brash and pretentious and here we are bickering like two queens or male canaries in their cage, spatting over females and some nothing bits of seed.

He says, 'I don't want to save the world, pretend to give a message to our patrons,' and he mimes primping at a ticket.

'Then what? It'll only ever be theatre, a masochistic evening out. They could be home, and drink or screw or watch TV,' and he laughs,

'They'll do all that, and less.'

I say, 'Then what?' again, although his anger runs up

my bones.

He says, 'You love that Faust role, think you sell your soul just once and wait the end that tells us not to try it, leads to hells, so better penitence and knee drill, maybe you'll get a sniff at some saintly broad, and see if you like that, a life of masturbation in the double tomb and tut tuts at the television,' and he stamps up our aisles, he screams, 'Yes, aisles, like in a church, and this you call a venue, where the burghers come for titillation and a flash of tits – what a monster we've invented, worship of humanity, of us, ourselves!'

He turns away: 'This awful hangar, with its no planes, no airmen, its barebone seats, no curtain that fell down – here, here I'll reveal the mirror. Behold the Man!'

It's true, if hell should have an antechamber, this is it, and who in hell's supposed to clean and decorate, there's tougher work to do, though I suppose the best there is, that's the best that we can do. 'It's stark, I like it stark,' I say.

'Why can't you give them satin, like to sit in, touch of gold and cupids, maybe some heating, make it worth their while,' and I am sure he wants to gas them, and I think there could be problems.

'Beneath your feet, Milan,' he says, 'and not just in the sewers. You should learn, but not from looking.'

'Be careful the bustle doesn't drown out the content,' I say.

'I don't have any content yet. Besides, people remember the peaks, not the geology.'

'People remember falling down the lavatory stairs in the interval.'

'Then we'll bring those stairs into the auditorium, everyone will have a void before them. And no intervals.'

I wish he didn't force me into Doctor Faustus's part. He's just the chance that everything happens to. The guy who only has bad hands and cannot bluff.

*

(*much later*)
This actor guy, Bruno, says, 'I've been fired. Igor says I get in the way of his ideas.'

'I'll try, get you back in, but I can't cover you.'

'You're too weak.'

'Experience tells me ...'

'You continue making the same mistakes. You can't rent a backbone at your age.'

I speak to Igor. He says, 'He interrupts my ideas. Yes, he's a bright lad, that's the trouble. The critical grin is not a useful adjunct to the muse's diadem.' He laughs.

'Aren't you exaggerating, trivialising? It's only a spectacle, a masque, not real power, real victims.'

'Then you haven't understood what we are doing here.'

I report to Bruno.

A while later, I see him with the crew. He calls me over.

'I went to the Bright Stars.'

'Good for you. What did they ask of you.'

'Nothing. Errands.' He's pushing a worn-out motor scooter.

It seems that almost all the crew have spare-time duties with the Bright Stars. Mostly, a crew's like a volcano – spits fire and rumbles, never lets you forget it stands there over you – then once in a lifetime, it erupts and covers you with sulphurous crap.

There's an intercom between my office and the stage. I needn't tell them I always leave it open. I ask one of the lads from below – now short hair, long hair don't have philosophical meanings, I can't say which one it was, but maybe Bic? – 'Who let you guys use this space?'

'Igor. It's just space.'

'What you do here? Deal? Wheel, maybe,' and to lighten the air I point to a scooter being serviced.

In the gloom there seems to be a Mercedes beneath that plastic.

'We don't want the Good Ones charging rent,' I say. We call the extractors, business, mafia – call them anything except that last one – we call them Good Ones, they're like the silent Fates who knit, the silent, blind monkeys who can break your legs or torch your house.

Bic says, 'Nah! Rubbish! Nothing here to interest. We're the Bright Stars, no one troubles us.'

I'm quite relieved: 'What are you, then? An agency?'

He laughs, 'Yes. We're agents. Ready for anything. Any service.'

*

Igor makes the actors rehearse with deafening music breaking over them. Pieces from the beginning and end of the world – quite similar, these, the first humans, laments for the ensuing massacres, rites of spring, field masses, masses for the dead, apotheoses and sacrifice – never less than eight horns and triple woodwind. In my office it sounded like heavy silver chains poured down marble steps, the cogs in my ears tangled together.

The actors first screamed, then mouthed, some cried with frustration. Igor sat hunched in the last row of seats, unmoved while the actors stood on boxes, put high wigs and helmets on their heads, found tall boots, tore off their clothes. Plaster and cement fell from the ceiling and I saw long rusty wires swaying to the screams of trumpet and the discharges of big drums.

'Leave the debris where it falls,' he said quietly when assistants tried to remove the rubble. I thought of the shy people, often reluctant and distracted, who might come to his shows, avoiding the crusts of plaster as though they were integral to whatever extravagant and bewildering show they were to see – I suppose for Igor they made the picture, he proposed smashing down the roof, already condemned and wilting, leaving the audience to stand in the rubble or improvise themselves a seat. And all this before the invention started. We lost many actors. Those that were left hated us.

'What if it rains?' I asked him, knowing he hated to get wet. That saved the roof project, but he was passionate for destruction, more even than destruction.

I said, 'You can get their attention by starting thirty minutes late and closing the bar in intervals.' A mistake.

'Attention? I don't want their attention, I want their suffering. If they must be drunk, so be it – give them each a bottle – meths, if you like. Make them howl, go blind. Share the pain of those idiots screaming their faces off up there,' he shouted, as the orchestra roared on and the half-naked sinners gestured and waved their fists on stage.

Igor's play. Nonhumanist, not destined for the future, or for future successes.

*

The public can decide – do you want rescue, plus the danger of death? Permanent suspension in the theatre? Or try to do a deal with people seeking death – and so, revenge? Do you want the resisters, in one way or another, to succeed? What might that mean, how far on is the future?

With some hindsight, how far is public interest, even public justice, with the martyrs? And a 'victory'?

Or is the idea of choice absurd, misleading and deceptive? Who has choices here? Buy the ticket, take your chance, then maybe have a vote or two, will of the majority, all that. And put it in a theatre, give it a frame, as if something is resolved, decided here – a place where gods and madmen rampaged, our blood myths acted out, or culture burned like acid etching, under that midday sun, on marble seats. All the human condition, your state, my state, incest, suicide and murder – the hope, the choice that's all around us – though not when it is useful. And when it's useful – whose is the use? Another slippery question – Igor might pose them all, but he sees resolution not in the arguments, but in the noise. And he's quite right – those stun grenades, the deafening tapes, the gunfire – everything's too loud to hear whether execution was by bullet or by poison. Noise everywhere.

*

I say, 'No shooting in my theatre,' and Dan, the carrier, Bright Star, hears me and laughs.

'It's all changed,' he confides. 'All the politics, new worlds, left, right, jackboots and flags in primary colours – all past. The only transgression, the only transformation, is the one that we propose. New life! All these creatives, slaves to managers, the business, production of whiffs of culture – what's their purpose, their future? Inventors – forced into the first stop, the bank, guy in the suit. Or gal. Which is worse? And the young punks, millions of them – timid thugs, guys who'd want to make giant strides but can't afford the trainers. What does mister middle ground, the Lady Aspiration, have to say to them, poor ruined kids – desperate at fifteen, shagged out at twenty, obese at thirty, forty, fifty – what boneyard is their destiny?'

He gestures at my auditorium, its slabs of bitumen. 'It's junkie death, this. It's where life puts the needle in its toes, and hopes the end is near, and warm and faceless,' and he laughs again.

I say, 'Don't the heavy guys give you trouble? I said no shooting here,' and Dan goes on, 'Those brain dead! Read the bible, do their accounts. Money and first communions, shooters and lots of jail, cell rules – lifetimes of managing the family, scum capitalism, ugly cretins making the beautiful suffer,' and on he goes.

'No shooting, mind,' I say again.

'Don't worry – we are his devilish majesty's most loyal and fragrant opposition. The dirty stuff is done outside – and doesn't matter. It's not our aim. We're not a business, don't want prisoners or slaves.'

'But not exactly legal,' I add, and again he laughs, 'To find if what we've done's illegal would take a hundred years, and laws from every level. Those old guys, the mafiosi, are so visible – whores in doorways, sniffing in the toilets, pistols trading round the trashcans. We aim at high invisibility – of ourselves, and what we do – the rest is just the dirty detail.'

Marco – I find he's the visionary, boss – takes over.

'Consider all the traditions, the patriarchy, nations, all that. Well, we've never been a nation, and never wanted it, so that does away with deference and obedience, the benevolence of the powerful – other myths like that. But mostly other people aspire to some immense idea – submission to that great dead thing, belief that any grain of sand can call itself a beach – or else they wonder why they got a state but still feel powerless and oppressed. The great idea – they can't even contemplate it. For them, it's trial and error, advantages or water cannon in the streets. Mere pragmatism. Protection. Any gang can give you justice and protection – maybe some cash as well.'

He's a beaky, streaky, yellowy lad, a savant. 'And the violence – men against women, men on men,' he rolls along. 'Where does all that come from, where's it going? Here, we still love children, or pretend to, most of our neighbours fear and hate them – nasty little knowalls, or they're armed and creeping up on you. So, where's all that ending up? And sex – all that stress on "afterwards", "despite". People get it over, off on their journeys – think of it as much as possible – but do it quickly, sniff some powder, take some drinks, to fix it in your memory, but at the time it's just a wave of culture crashing down. Throws you on the rocks, it's good it's over, then to think of something else, dream some more dreams. But all this worship of your body – leads to every heresy and then to disbelief. The body dies – it's mostly spent its life to die and turn to marbled flab.'

I barely understand. I say, 'It's all quite eloquent – but after all, you're just a gang. The old stuff dies, and more stuff – well, I can't say "takes its place", the picture changes, other forms move in, and on. But gangs are gangs – quite interstitial.'

He shudders a little at this last word. He strokes it, holds it up, tests its opacity. Then, offhanded, says, 'Well, the future's all made up of little bits, but when it comes, it's all there is, you have to cling to it although it runs away like water.'

Gangs. Find a gang and join. Find a gang that wants to take you. Stick to the rules, pull onward like a donkey. Then into the mincer, with the rest.

Marco turns away from me, he's found me wanting, or maybe tires of finding words.

*

'Whose little lamb are you?' I ask. It's a sad and serious girl, one of their flock.

She doesn't answer directly, but says, 'I'm Elektra. Grandfather was a positivist, wanted the kids called Voltage, Radium and so on, but mother insisted on a classical name, so I'm part energy, part sadness.'

'And a question of matricide too' – which is all I remember of Elektra's story, though I don't believe in original sin, and there's no certainty that she'll act out the drama of her name, although it usually happens so. Behind us a screen tells us the nation's leader's charged with paedophilia.

'Well, there go the judges,' I say. 'He's been grooming his people for decades, and now he'll never go to trial,' but she seems indifferent.

'At least he's got the common touch,' she says, but without enthusiasm.

Above us there's a shriek. Factory whistle. 'Only the avant garde uses that sound,' I say. 'It's quite out of fashion in our industries,' and I hear Igor try it over and over. I ask her,

'I'm curious – how do you see your boyfriends' industry?'

'Taking over brains? Clever.'

'And the punishment? That they deal out?

She laughs, 'Everyone has a right to self-defence. Anyway, what I care about is painting,' and she unfurls her folder.

I'm thankful the drawings are nonverbal, quite figurative, indeed. Even kitsch. Even ... I almost say 'quite good', but other people's creation encountered by chance is always a delusion when it's not a masterpiece.

I say, 'Masterpiece used to mean the start of a career, now it means the summit, or the end. So maybe it doesn't mean that much at all,' but she folds them away, not bothered.

Igor is reading a book on tigers – lucky tigers and dangerous tigers. He has read many books on shape-shifting, and I see his actors swell and float, for them bi-location is quite easy – they're often outside smoking and inside screaming, they're like distended lungs, bellies of bagpipes, leather sacks hairy inside. Their voices are monstrous, no longer voices but the echoes from basilicas, shouts of dying animals sacrificed – becoming part of the mystery, horribly martyred.

'Can't scale that down,' says Bic, poking his index fingers into brains, quite soundless. Electronic. 'Respect for that training,' he says, of drawing, tigers, who's to tell – as if it's training greyhounds chasing electric fluff. 'What does it achieve?'

Elektra says, 'You make the loudest sound you can, and then it's happiness, maybe, or some other resolution, like – make a precipice – you can jump off or fly, or just then turn away.'

That's the idea, but why? Why the precipice?

Mondays the Bright Stars sell some stuff. Not robbed, just counterfeit, but Marco says, 'It's fakes of fakes, it's fashion rage. Copies. What you want,' and Dan nods, 'There's no aura, if that's what you mean.'

I say, 'I don't mean anything. Just intrigued.' And quite ensnared.

*

On other days, they are an agency, and people come and sit on office chairs and go out pleased, some papers printed out by Bic. And then there's the commissions. To transit stuff, by ship or raft, people or phrases, estimates, it's all the same, it all goes by the wire – and none of it is specially real, except perhaps the people, but Marco says, 'Those are the ones you never see, who never tell. You never count, and they don't do the sums – its benefaction, in whatever sense,' and I don't know what sense, although I know you're better off not being here, or there, and maybe pay a guy to take you up a ladder, throw a six and cross a desert, fool the cops. And anywhere is better at this time than where you are, and so you pay to make a move, some day you'll reach the board's end and become a king or queen, or own your territory, even sleep a bit – but in the meantime, on you must move, and if the Bright Stars don't feel like doing it, then someone else, some thug, some clod – that's what they say – will take your cash and put two fingers in your eyes or lock you in the fridge, or just forget you on some island, waiting for a boat. Boat in a bottle.

They're a fascinating bunch, and their beautiful hens,

Elektra, Franca, Giulietta – painted like Copts and cooing round – they're each one an epic of aspiration and good taste. Monday's taste.

I tell Igor, 'They're remarkable lads. They know the past, they're our future.'

He ignores me. 'I have the shape, the sound. It's the content that eludes me. I know all the sounds and smells. Fear. Noise.'

'Yes, I've heard the noise.'

'Sitting in the theatre. The fucking theatre, man! Then in come the martyrs, and you're pressed into your own – martyrdom – at their hands, for what? Crimes done in your name. And in come the saviours, your guys – and they're going to kill you. Design. Or accident that comes right from your horrible history,' and I add, 'Everyone's horrible history.'

'Specific, this one,' he says, 'and everyone's at once in touch with it, crime and expiation, crime you never did, expiation that can't work, would be obscene.'

I say, 'I know – putting the art in's hard.'

*

A scientific gang. Their purposes? To enter brains, change humans and their nature, nature too. To punish. To profit. To protect – mostly themselves. 'We are the fantasists, the others are clods.'

Cultivate traditional foods. Win the love of beautiful women (I've seen them – Elektra, Franca, Giulietta – all not bad!)

Four stars, and thugs to help us out. Marco, poet. Dan the carrier, runs the agency, Johnny the fixer, patron of the thugs, and Bic the Laptop who looks through everyone's keyhole.

Poet? Or visionary, the old roles, sentimental, you can bet. Even happy families, blood weddings, all that, aspiring to the petty bourgeoisie, intelligence that works on just a paragraph, commonplaces made graffiti, fixed for everyone to see and to ignore. Disgusting, can't we pay some cleaners, maybe a guard with gun and radio? But here the content too eludes us.

*

Beneath Igor and the theatre, the Bright Stars work. No shooting here, I beg you, please. 'We aren't the thugs. We are the future.'

What's beneath them? A realm beneath their basement. That they know about. Everything is built on something else, no licence, just obsolescence, forgetfulness. To be the thing you worship, or you say you do – but here – a lack of content. Igor's shocking, empty statements.

'Are you badged? Badged to me?' I ask Katya.

'Badged like "pinned", like branded ox? If you like. If it makes you happy.'

'The Bright Stars' women talk like that. And the guys say, "Tonight I'm going badging."'

She's unimpressed: 'So, what's new? Little curds of tradition, help the water flow.'

I think 'hmm', and say, 'Igor's making it up as he runs,' and she replies, 'Everyone does.'

'He went down well – somewhere. Came recommended.'

'The best, the only way.'

I say to Marco, later, 'I should know what you're

doing down there.'

'We'll pay rent,' he says, 'more rent.'

'OK.'

He tells me without being asked, 'Everything new starts with a gang – family, dynasty, great saint, preferably from some grave – gang or clan. Few years to make it stick, bit of capital, soldiers, execution of the traitors,' he pauses and laughs. 'The corporations, the long wars – a hundred years, thirty years, cold wars, wars of religion – they're especially bountiful. In the end, all run by gangs.'

'It seems obvious. Now you say it.'

'When you peel back the rhetoric, yes. Stuff like "you voted for them, it's the system, progress, liberation," whatever the fuck, and everyone wanting to be rich and normal, push the stowaways overboard. Plenty of sharks around.' And he laughs. They're always laughing. He says, 'That Igor makes a good noise – he's on to trumpets and synthesisers now. Hope in the end it's worth it all.'

I'm concerned. I say, 'He's patterning in the public. Where they'll sit. Role for each. Put them in the scene. Sitting there, waiting for death. Paying their money.'

'Well,' he says, 'It's too much of a scam for me. But you'd better watch him and your Katya. If he can't get to write his play, he may take on your woman, if you care, of course. He's always putting her on those elastics, naked, flying out over the seats, what there's left. Bit of fantasy playing there.'

Marco dreams his future. 'Wow, like the king and queen in Egypt, high over the dam.'

I ask, 'Who's to be queen?'

'They're not even touching, king and queen. I might be on my own. Like the presidents on the mountain –

though I'd prefer a whole body. With tattoos.'

'You've got to be dead,' I say sourly, though kings and presidents don't bother me, don't mean a lot.

'Well, that's something we can change quite easily. Just to sit there, forever, watching the guys drink the water in the dam, till it's all gone and wasted, and I'm still there, father to the people. Mother too.'

*

Not long after, a lump of bitumen falls. It's very near, and as I skitter away, other lumps follow in a line. I say to Johnny, 'Hey, you're the fixer. You trying to fix me? Maybe because I'm Serbian?'

'Serbian,' he says, 'what's the link? Some kind of religion? If someone wants to get you, you'll get got. Better carry an umbrella – a steel one. This place isn't stable.'

I say, 'Maybe some guy's play got turned down. You guys haven't aspirations that way, have you?' Almost everyone has quires of unpublishable stuff, for movies, theatres, you name it and it all goes as garbage on the web. But behind it all, there's a good thrust of jealousy and delusion – just like for genocides, only usually the writer's short of weapons, and I'm thankful for that, though if the roof falls in we'll maybe lose our licence – then I think, well, no, we'll get a licence from the Bright Stars – they'll just want to put their plays on, or their girlfriends', what the hell, if no one comes their cut's reduced, and maybe someone sees a little sense – and then I think of Igor. Not a Noh play, just a no, and though I'm scared by falling stuff, I snigger just a bit to give our Johnny time to smarten up, but then, if it was him he'll try again, nothing ventured, as the bankers say. Though what's the gain for him, I just don't know – money in the art line being just all air and speculation, not even Igor's seating plans can make it solid – though if he should eliminate an audience, that would be solid trouble, not to mention hell.

In the basement, Elektra is painting. Four easels. Haven't seen so many for years. The Bright Stars posing, singly, fooling about, as sacred knots, intertwined turtles, apes in paradise. She's scolding them, shaking them. They're hooting with invention.

'These will go,' says Dan with pomp, 'all over the world, to all affiliates,' and Marco adds, 'A touch of divinity will do no harm.'

She uses black like Beckmann. Her effect lies between the elevated and the threatening.

'How will the Kazaks respond to this,' Bic asks, 'You'd better put in something showy, like a Cadillac, a park with bridges, some good cutlery,' and she ignores him. But the idea is planted, and she adds to some – tattoos, and others have accessories, a holster on the table, watch that tells your mood.

And I feel scruffy, and I think of where my grandparents were born, that single street, red peppers drying, pig shit an affront to neighbours – if they cared. Grim dancing followed by grim coupling, the horse bought with your sweat, horse dying so much worse than people. Kids that save your name, your land, and eat you to the bone.

The Bright Stars go first class, or else incognito – but they go everywhere, passports a gazetteer. 'Lots of initiatives on this little fellow,' says Bic – he trips in space and lands in Mexico, Shanghai.

'I can see the future,' Johnny hums, 'and no one's any

older, no one dies,' it's banal, but I think, 'They should be doing Igor's play. They are Igor's play,' and from above I can hear Katya protesting, as she's launched again, 'Igor, I'm a dancer, not a blob on an elastic!'

Perhaps, if an actor's just a container, of no particular size or colour, a dancer's something else, is body-bound, unfree, a double, not a void. But Igor likes to empty anything, or any person, takes the musicians' instruments, makes them make sounds like something else – or no sounds at all, miming some riff, some rhythm. Improvising from the spaces in their heads. They hate him, he has voided them, but he has gained nothing, taken nothing from them. He despises what little content they may have – the music, air, they breathe and strum for him must just be vacuum. From nothing, something grows. Or else it doesn't.

We're at the primal stage, when Bright Stars are away – Cancun, Nagpur. Elektra's pictures tour the world – to be affiliate, you have to stick one on your wall. Like a famous person, though they're just about unrecognisable. Elektra says, 'I only paint the kings,' with that she's done. Finished. Passed on the gift.

*

Marco asks about the play to come. I tell him, 'It's got the most beautiful, magnificent frame ever. Just lacks the picture,' and I think of Katya. When I speak of her, I talk from the heart – a funny metaphor, all you want of the heart is that it goes on beating.

Marco says, 'I don't go for beautiful things – it just means someone got there first. Like saying things are untouched when they're on the tourist track and full of belvederes.'

'Do you recognise magnificence?'

'That's better – but it could be an Edsel, or something quite trite and fleeting.'

I say, 'If you think like that it must be hard to do poetry.'

'The others call me Poet. I'm just a visionary.'

I think of a picture of dervishes, having a good time, being massaged, drinking, reaching into tall jars for dates. Ready to whirl, but not just now.

At least these guys don't hate Serbians, don't know where it is, it was. And those real socialists, the true, the just – where are they now? An invention unpublished, obsolete before you translate the paper model into metal, real metal.

*

Johnny handles the political cover. 'Those guys are interested in cheese and pigeon shit,' he says. 'So, that deals with serving the people – and the rest is vanity. Theirs, and ours. That's what people want – sell and eat the cheese, clean up the shit. The rest is power unscrutinised. It keeps them, if not happy, off our backs and fawning too.'

News comes of a shooting. Dan says, 'The guy is selling houses – stuck in a jam, he pulls his piece and pop – high on the shoulder, guy in front, some sporty type. Better to be enclosed,' and Johnny says, 'Those guys who sell the houses – very angry types. Like travel agents. Get frustrated. Random pops, and once in jail, they don't know what to do. We love them,' and he laughs. They make the cops look good, arresting them. Little snubby guns, lucky to hit a human.

Johnny says, 'We'll clear the dogs tomorrow.'

'I haven't heard them,' I say. Who could hear anything with Igor and his show? Johnny says, 'The Romanians get to stay a bit, they're in the space down the downstairs.'

'I didn't know there was,' I say.

'Well, for them it's an adventure and besides, that too will pass, we'll make them rich and clear them out – they can't stay with the dogs, we can't put them on the street – besides, they're always relatives of yours.' He questions as he affirms.

I say, 'Not me, maybe ancestors. Common use of the horse, displacing infantry, but little more, not language and not bosses, sometimes occupiers we shared,' but Johnny's off in politics.

'Those guys are real antiquaries,' he says. 'Show them a shrine, a scrawl, bundle of bones, skulls to roll – and they're protecting them, consultants – all that stuff, and then the tourists come, they make a mess and then there's millions cleaning up and guarding them, and payoffs to this church and that, but oh so slow, and little sums, and notes in envelopes. You need to live a hundred years to turn a buck, and long before, they lose it all to keep them out of jail,' he laughs. For clients in the basement –

'And then, I think we need a desk,' he says, 'though two chairs seems a bit more cosy, and another Merc to keep the other company.' And they have that red tank.

It's interesting, and I don't hold him back.

*

Then on my intercom we hear, 'What you see in that dreary bastard?' It's Igor and Katya, Katya isn't keen to defend me, just says ho hum, and Igor tells her that the show will make her body sparkle – and an actor comes to me and says, 'That Igor's fired me, says I can't scream loud enough – it's not our job, the scream comes, if it does, spontaneously.'

I tell him, 'I can do nothing – he's the boss, it's just auditions,' but the guy is clearly miffed, he says, 'Igor'll give everyone like me a ticket. In the audience,' and I think, 'If the show goes as it's planned, this guy'll have no trouble screaming,' and Dan and Johnny look at me, a little kindly, and they say, 'Come on, we'll give you a ride,' off the Merc the plastic goes and we are in and whirling off.

*

The fat black car speeds up – a cop gives chase for fun, then waves as he drops out. We're bouncing mostly up and down, and on the down we hit the tarmac, but as he races on, Dan says, 'They only made a few like this, looks like a slug, flies like a carpet,' and I think, 'Really, the politicians covering for them – they can't be small-town mayors, worried about the cheese. That red tank – just a souvenir, can't make a coup with just one piece of antique armour,' but Johnnie says, 'It's red because the last guy painted it like that,' and it makes me think – 'If there's mystery behind some scene, it means you can't take it seriously,' and on we run.

We're on the outskirts now, the sheep are grazing on grey grass, the water here in pools is blue and silver, yell-ow, sage, it's really beautiful, and Johnny says, 'You shouldn't eat the cheese,' and here are viaducts, arches for triumphs in the future, roads from nowhere, and a hub of industry, the guards with pistols playing cards, the sheds all fallen in.

We're closer in – and Johnny says, 'The dealers keep the music loud', and as we pass the snaking blocks, each palace has a window pouring down the Heavy Metal, just like slag, to get the clients in. And now we're into gangland, little kingdoms – surveillance, some by squads of little boys, others have fat cars parked on the corners with inside four guys. I wonder how, with those dark shades, they see what's what – their cars have deeply tinted windows, but Dan says, 'It's just for show – one day we might use the red tank, take it round, to show them what we think,' but what they think is mystery.

We're near the centre now, and there's a press of tourists, pickpockets, and security – they're all looking down and backwards – yes, I guess there's architecture, how'd you tell, and maybe florid paintings and the stuff that you can't steal or do your writing on, and Johnny says, 'There, you've seen it all, and saved the pain of travelling,' though pain there is, of speed and wanting to be finished with it.

But Dan has seen the cinemas – we all remember movie time and chat like antiquarians of when we had our lives inside. He says, 'The story business – that was one magnificent scam! Horror and love, night-flying, massacres – those old magicians and their mates – how they invented! Made you weep, and rage, and marvel – it was all an art! Or maybe you never thought – they twist your tail, they take your cash, they give you fantasy eternal. Didn't you see it?'

'I see it,' and I'm back with Igor, and I hear him say

to Katya, ‘Your mister “itch”, the guy without an origin, you know the joke, “You can take the itch out his pants but you’ll never take the ‘itch’ off his name.”’ And that’s maybe Katya’s laughter, though usually with me she is quite delicate, but now, who knows, and I feel nauseated, Dan is saying, ‘The countryside. It doesn’t smell, but then it gets you in the throat. You shouldn’t eat that cheese.’

Johnny says, ‘Who’d ever want to be big boss of that kind of place?’ and Dan says, ‘Spinning money out of junk.’

‘And the *people*, my dear,’ laughs Dan.

‘The bosses there are all illegals, spend their lives in hiding, making people sad – just parasites and chancers. Who’d want that – unless you’ve extended families to support, and more fool you. All that responsibility, and then some punks will shoot you dead,’ and Johnny makes the gesture, finger cocked then smoking.

‘The trick’s all in the switching, the planes; from dust to diamonds. And on balance – we are benefactors, explorers. Not for the recognition, that absurdity – no, it’s the creation.’ And Dan smiles round, half serious.

What do they do – or rather, what’s the part they think enriches them?

Igor tells me, later, ingratiating – ‘I’ve got the emotions to the boil. I’m getting there.’

*

I overhear Katya say to Elektra: ‘A little while here, then we could go away. Even together ...’ and Elektra says, ‘Dan thinks that even before it was all fashion and celebrity, it was just a scam. Writers drawing it all out, making it all a fiction, making you laugh and cry – not a reflection but a travesty. He says that all that's interesting is *faisandage* – the hanging of the dead, the corruption, the pheasant whiff that makes it good. To eat, of course. The smell of death that makes desirable the lovely bird, that stimulates.'

Katya says, 'Well, Dan sounds quite smart.'

'He did a bit at college, we all did. It doesn't cost here. But it's Bic that's really bright – that laptopping leaves you free to put the content in, invent. Pity that you're empty, as an actor,' and Katya says, 'The dance just makes a thing, quite odourless, for guys to fantasise about. Same guys that patronise your paintings, maybe buy a bit of you to go with,' and Elektra says, 'That Igor – just can't spit it out.'

'He's a spectator, wants to do it all, but really he can only see someone else who does it. Even reality. He's in the wrong place – he should be buying tickets, not selling them,' and they both laugh – it's clear that Katya doesn't dwell on me, but surely likes it when they look at her.

Igor tells me, 'The Bright Stars want to take me for a spin – a bit grander than yours!'

*

Dan and Johnny, off again. Marco stays, to work with Laptop. I ask him, 'Why all this marble?'

'For the clients. For the Romanians. For us. We found it in the grottoes underneath the underneath. I hate Roman painting, umber and faded purple, the gods long gone, the alabaster cracks up when you move it.'

I say, 'You're supposed not to take it, and to hide it if you do. And how do you know the gods have gone?'

Dismissively, he says, 'Who thinks of Cybele now? My favourite. The cults were meant to be concealed. And now they are, for good.'

I say, 'Like Katya. She's gone. I feel sore about it.'

'Roll with the fashion. While you're living it, you have to feel the quality – it'll soon wear out. Unless you're wedded to the antique business. Enjoy the ups, you won't suffer through the downs.' I say, 'It's not impermanence I resent, it's betrayal.'

With that he seems to sympathise. 'It's all that Russian's fault. Destroyer.'

'Only the name's a bit of Russian. He's just a tormented soul, handing out the suffering.'

'He makes one hell of a noise', and I think, the Bright Stars, with those Heavy Metal tapes, everything roars, the rock is like a gruyère, sound spurtling out like whale spume, tunnels of the Underground alive with riffs and shouting.

Marco says, 'That Katya's done her sums, and she'll be off. Dancing like a dervish, without the spirituality.'

And I'd like to ask, where does the money come from, and he's saying, 'Bic, the laptop guy, can tell us what the tall poppies, the big cheeses, plan to do – so we do the crit., the next steps too.'

'So you're super lobbyists, consultants?'

'We know the future. Sell a longer term. Or keep it for ourselves.'

'That sounds quite legal.'

'Depends – everyone has some secrets – some you can find out, others not. It's poker with appeals courts, scams overseen by guys in robes. Roman imperial, I'd say.'

'And so – you make the future?'

'Men make their history – you may have heard of that? – but only within the limits. Limits we don't recognise. Then – there's our charitable work.'

I think of the red tank. 'Employment for the lost boys?'

'Where the cash is made.'

I remember something about men changing circumstances, and needing to educate the educator – it must mean Igor and myself. And it goes on, that this divides society into two parts, 'one of which is superior to society'. That must be the Bright Stars. It's a heavy message.

*

Igor returns from his spin, burnished like a copper cockbird.

He enthuses, 'They took me up so high – mountains like gingerbread, each with a scholar and a winebowl, stretched out in the sun. And on every rock a gazelle, so slender it seemed made of tin, and seas – red, yellow, green, and forests without trees, just universes of insects, hierarchies of wing and leg, moving up and down, great heaving masses and all cooperating – some were feeding the young of others, warrior ants defend them all, and birds – songs like huge orchestras of brass, they sing together – roses, reunions, sweet farewells.'

His face is red and beaming. I ask, 'Where did you go?'

'Everywhere and nowhere. All connects, everything is so familiar, so many times lived over, drained to its dreg and yet eternal. And I was me, and other people, my name was mine, and also uncles, cousins, Russians, and we were all flying together – deserts with a surf of green, moustaches of scrub, and ochre wind towers – and the books! The lost plays! Menander in Arabic, all complete, and actors down there spouting it all out, no more zeros to be coloured in, but solid, some with orange, some with purple, wigs,' and Marco says, 'They must have given you something to calm your guts before they took you off,' and Igor says,

'Oh well, I don't remember, you mean like a cake that says "now eat me" like the book? I can't imagine that,' and he goes on and on, and Marco says, quite kindly, 'We had hoped to help you with your play. And may it run a thousand years,' and I think, 'Yes, it would help the Bright Stars if Igor were a fixture here,' and Marco turns to me as Igor rants and twists,

'Those old civilisations – it's so sad – with all that endeavour all they've left us is their magic. And they've left a world where everything's connected, those old warriors are moving through us, their nothing hands put weapons in our hands, they goad us on, the priests have no truth left, but only magic, rituals, the blood sacrifice repeated every week, we drink it in, are stupefied. Are stupid – not a critic nor an agent we.'

'And this lack of place, the lack of happening?' I ask.

'We're all in one world, we slide across it – it's a billiard ball and we invent its features. Make them. Shift the rivers, mountains, dry the seas. And do you think the people are all solid in their bodies? Think of the schools, to make us all the same, the wars, the genocides, we're bundled into graves with all our friends, our comrades raise their guns, and our last song is sung, and then it's sung again, and put on tape, on ether, and there's our sound, it lives for ever. But we don't.'

He's caught Igor's rush, and I ask again, how do they

make their cash. 'We sell them the consequences of their projects. We see their futures, as they make them, but before they happen. Laptop can do it, only he's a guy that's difficult to pin down. Obscure, even.'

I say, 'No one pays to know their futures. If they can't correct their projects, what's the point? No one pays to know that life is tragic, that you make mistakes – or even that you win, because I'd take your lead and halve and halve again your winnings. No one will pay for that.'

'Then we make them pay.'

I ask, 'What's this about the future, Marco? What's the attraction, what kind of place is it? Is it a place? Does anything happen there? What sense does it make?'

'It's quite familiar. Only you're not there. And so it's quite unfamiliar. And you're not there. You must imagine that little clay figure, when God says, "Very clever, but it's not alive," and you say, "Of course not, how could it be? But tomorrow, if it's not been junked, it'll be there, and people will say it's magic, and it won't be alive, and I and maybe You – we won't be alive either. And that's the future, all that you know and don't about it."'

He goes on, 'Laptop can have you see a lot of little true things on a screen. Remember all those revolutions that they used to make? The betrayals, sacrifices, and all that determination. To make us see that we are all one species. But we are, we were, we will be – all one species. That's the future too.'

I say, 'That's quite depressing.'

'That's too bad.'

I say, 'What's your role in that? To be alive. Live in the future. Have a fine gang. And money, power and women – for the straight guys. Pretty much the same for gays. The rest is speculation. Or Sufism.'

*

(*a little later*)
All four are twirling machetes, it looks like the old Peking opera, or dervishes, but not nice, not kind. ‘Are we enjoying this?’ Johnny exhorts, and they laugh. Bruno is skating round the walls, sometimes he tweaks at the door, but knows it’s tight, he doesn’t speak or maybe even think of crying out, as if the sound might show the others where he is.

Marco, the poet, skids into his path, and as Bruno raises an arm to defend, slices off his fingers, and I hear them plop.

There is a cheer, and now the noise is like hounds baying, and Bruno at bay screams,

‘Fuck you, fuck you all,’ and like a magistrate Bic says, ‘No, that was in your cesspit mind, to fuck my beautiful sweet girl. The thought is heavier than the deed – a deed you’d never have been up to, more’s the point,’ and Dan the carrier says, quite thoughtful, ‘If we don’t discipline the thoughts, when the actions happen, we’d be lost. And that poor girl would be a victim – ah, if only she had innocence to lose, but that she’s lost a while ago, so now there’s just the violence, or even worse, compliance. We’d even for a moment lose the girl, and then, my friend,’ the others laugh, ‘we’d have to take you in. Or maybe not. And she, poor girl, we’d have to punish her – and that would not be just, and so, you see that’s where a thought can take you,’ and Bruno holds what’s now his hand under his armpit, but the blood from spots is now a flow, and as he whirls, Johnny cuts off another section from the left and unprotected paw.

‘What roles now?’ shrieks Bic. ‘Theatre of cruelty,

when that comes round again,' and now the cuts come slow and deeper – part of a leg to slow him down, but they keep off the head, though there is Johnny at his cheek, maybe an eye is popped, there seems a lot of spit and tears and jelly from an eyeball, and he's making noises now that's not a scream but like actors on TV in situations they pretend are similar to this, a kind of chuckling, clucking, as he sees his proud body sectioned up – the touch, the sight, and now they're going for his sex, and I am silent here and watching to the end, I wouldn't dream of leaving, nor of closing eyes or throat, the throat is blocked and who would intervene against those Bright Stars – they're having an unstoppable good time, and Bic is over Bruno, he shouts, 'My girl, my fucking girl, you dirtied her with your obsessive pokey thoughts. We are the law, you goddam knew it and decided,' he swishes with his machete, 'to do your will, your little will against our power,' and now they're at the body and I'm sure the nipples now are sliced away, my body goes to slush in sympathy, the stomach next and something shoots right out, I think of sausages and quite nearly it is that, and they are on him, four of them get in each other's way, it's butcher's time, a kind of rhythm like a string quartet, the bows, machetes, sliding to and fro, they grunt although he must be dead, something avenged – but no, they leave him and he gives a last slow turn, just like a plane before it loses power and then I see that Dan's already rolling out a hose, to clean the place, and Bruno's gone – he's had his judgment day and hell and expiation all in one, and if there's talk of pardons I won't yield, but now what's left of Bruno is a sack, the kind they use for parcels, and I think, 'Who can I tell, and will the Bright Stars do the same to me, and maybe not, my role was not exactly glorious, nor yet decisive. And in a way they're right – they put him on the crew, and sure – he knew he had to keep his thoughts on theatre, not the women ... maybe he was too complicit, one of the gang, though a subordinate, and me – spectator but quite clean,' although – a speck of blood has penetrated even here, I nearly laugh, what crap symbolism's there! – but really I'm all shaken up, legs, throat, all that, are as they're said to be. Shaky.

A terrible event. Their lust, enjoyment, justice being done – and seen in silence. Fear of the same.

*

After his whirl round purgatory – it not being abolished, as they say, though it is true – as they say – there's no one in it, Igor produced a document.

Igor's document

Who remembers Chechnya? Who remembers the terrorists, and the Russians, watching the spectacle, a public in at its own death. The Chechens seeking vengeance, the Russians killed by their state and its protectors. My idea – the theatre, death, the public. Also present – terror all round, the state that provokes, that kills, dispenses justice, says what vengeance is just and which is punishable. And who remembers that, the name of the spectacle, the city, what became of Chechnya, who brought justice, who brought death and who brought neither, and who both. Yet it happened, all the media covered it, and now it's quite invisible, the paste behind the wallpaper.

And so I thought – that's the theatre. Forget the stage, the musical. The spectacle is the moment, life, death, observing, passive. Victim. Agent.

Then I got lost. Reality they say is never intricate and confused. But I was stuck.

And so I thought – let's take the actors – who are zeros. The dancers – who are bodies. The musicians – who make vibrations. Put them on the stage. And singers – who seem to speak and cry – and make us cry, though we don't speak – what do they have, the singers are like elves, or sprites, they can't be human, don't eat and drink, or deviate, or think – but yet they work in words, they 'speak' to us.

We'll put them all together – back on the stage. Forget the audience – a random bunch, distracted, sceptical, confused. 'What's all this stuff?' they think, 'I haven't – or I have – seen it all before.' And so I thought – the stage, the play.

*

Anatomy of error, Igor's vision blurring. Mere play. What's he done, I ask. A mountain, a farrago. It's all content, everything is happening, all is burnt and flooded, live bodies are carried here and there, the genocide's denounced, we mostly cry but sometimes laugh, we double up, we wish that we were dead, we wish that they were dead and so we needn't pity them, that goddam catharsis for crimes and criminals we shouldn't pardon – oh the tragedy of it all, we're in and out of it, well, yes, the incest and the matricide we enter in the spirit, then we're out again, ballets of paedophiles and forest creatures. What an imagination! Everything has happened and we're satisfied, the bar has closed but all around are bars and dancing clubs, and maybe there'll be sex or some new group.

*

So, Igor has a success, though not too many come, the crew is left without its pay, and no one suffers more than me, and every night it's Armageddon, and we wander from Dust City up the mountains, here's a ballet, ladies trying to be frogs, and there a prison or a work camp, and dust poured over us. And so it goes.

The Bright Stars think it's fun, and play their tapes, I hear Mercedes being revved, reality is all around – some people even clap.

There is great noise below, and Katya has disappeared. I ask the Bright Stars. Johnny jokes, she'll be back, cats wander off.

'Katya the shapeshifting poledancer,' says Dan.

Laptop adds, 'Katya the polecat,' but Marco says seriously, 'Katya's a tragic name,' and the rest are silent. He goes on – 'Exposure of her body – disposal of her body. It's all linked up,' mysteriously.

*

They all wear black T-shirts with white legends. They interchange, maybe to confuse – what, a witness? I see 'our present story is now ended,' Dostoevsky. '*Vienne la nuit sonne l'heure Les jours s'en vont je demeure*' Apollinaire, spelt wrong. '*Les yeux d'Elsa les yeux d'Elsa les yeux d'Elsa*', and Laptop wears, 'the bourgeois state without the bourgeoisie'.

'Well, I recognise that one,' I say.

'Well, you would,' Laptop says, 'you having been to school.'

Marco promises, 'We'll watch for her,' but I wish at least we had a body or a postcard. I see her walled up, in a trunk, even behind the marble, a goddess stepped in from the wrong fable – there's so much noise you couldn't hear a mew, my heart is beating like a pair of bongos, Igor's rehearsing for some new adventure, and I hear Johnny, he says, 'We had a vote regarding that politico.'

'How did it go?' I ask.

'I was against,' says Johnny, 'Marco for. Dan and Laptop both indifferent, so of course we did it. Tried it.'

Laptop says, 'We didn't care about the contract – sewers, was it, railways underground – the contacts at the top were what we wanted – Johnny said he felt it was a burden.'

'The guy's a super zero,' Johnny says, and Dan puts in, 'And Katya, as his friend – she should have oiled that deal right through.'

Later I say to Igor, 'I hope Katya didn't offend our young guests from the depths,' and he then turns on me, and says, 'You don't know how to treat a woman.'

'Certainly I don't! She didn't want treating anyway,' but then he rants against the Bright Stars – the noise, car fumes, the refugees, all for young punks ...

I say, 'They pay for us,' and he shouts on, that art should pay its way, if not, then the state and not some bunch of little criminals, but Katya's still unfound, unheard from, and I wish her dead, uncertainty resolved, and Igor gives her up at once from jealousy, and 'who's this guy she's friendly with, of course the Bright Stars wouldn't tell me.'

Everyone's reading headlines, 'Premier in teens love romp,' and the Bright Stars are censorious. 'The tarts didn't like their presents,' says Johnny. 'So beans got spilled.'

I insist with them about Katya, and a postcard arrives, it seems not in her hand ('Maybe she fell,' says Dan, solicitous) – it shows what may be the Cold Mountains, but we can't read the print and the stamp's been stolen. 'It's cold here, the mountains are high and cold. Here in the mountains, here one feels free. Do you remember, Katya.'

Remember what, I wonder, and I'm not convinced, but it's enough to calm me, and I think, 'The cops would take this as good evidence', so 'We're all happy now,' says Marco. 'And besides, you're foolish if you think politicos can cover you – they'll throw you off the sled for sure.'

And Igor says, 'Well, maybe she did want someone after all, not wanting me nor Milan, and not even our lads here. Now it's all up to Elektra, who can paint the scenes, and Giulietta can be heroine for once.'

'For Juliet she's very young – very young to act that part,' I say. I think, 'From revenger tragedy to Romeo – how can Igor think of such a leap?' but he's impatient.

'This is a play about pre-teens – think of all the males out there, they fantasise. I'm tired of shocking them – from shock to schlock I'll go!'

Well, Igor thinks he's some correctness to protect, integrity. It's a thing a plumber has, but in the theatre – it's all real, though if you get up on the stage and join in, you man of action, you'll find it's real within a hedge.

Igor goes on, staggering a little under his inspiration. 'Franca will be Romeo. Besides, Giulietta's only young as an actress – she's just the right age for fantasy. And Elektra too will be Romeo – give it a little weight. The real Elektra kept things in the family – hung up on her brother, wasn't it, something about the mother? Anyway, three women for two parts – will satisfy the critics.'

'It sounds a hoot. Indeed, a pre-teen love romp.'

'I've got big roles too – for the Bright Stars, especially for Marco. He'll be Mercutio.'

I object, 'I don't think they'll want to play themselves in public. They'll be paying you to make them act,' and I think of all that non-union labour, coming in cheap and losing us the crew.

I say, 'A great discovery for the theatre maybe, but exposing them in such a tawdry way ...'

He considers this: 'Can't think why they go for such young chicks. Of course, the best age here is fourteen, fifteen, then they start to calculate.'

I say, 'The Bright Stars aren't in the love and cuddles business,' and I think how after every masterpiece, the great creators try a Romeo, and Igor says, 'We'll let this one sit and simmer, then,' but meanwhile things are happening and the Bright Stars brightly shine.

I tell Igor, 'They're warriors, they don't do theatre,' and maybe that's why it's incongruous to tell the police about them. Cops and warriors? Besides, all have their battle plans. Igor says,

'Dan's a driver. Bic – Laptop's – a hacker. Warriors – I don't think! As for you, you listen in to everyone. Where's your discrimination?'

I say, 'If you eliminate the warriors, you've all the so-called innocents, women and children in our society – hanging around and telling tales. Best eliminate the innocents – too many kids anyway, all aspiring warriors, and any woman here can look after a fistful of kids.'

Igor says, 'It's true the women spy. But I hear the Bright Stars had some trouble with a weedy guy, some Bruno. Spying. You'd better watch yourself. And Katya too.'

Who spies for who, I wonder, and was it Katya that I wanted, or was it just that she was wantable and free? And I laugh at this – we're back in Romeo land, where not getting what you want is still a tragedy. And later, Marco says, giving himself more weight,

'I think we bridge it all. We're clearly of the right, but of course, the social right, coming from the social depths, I might say the dregs. You see the working stiffs, goddammit, how they work – and cry into their pasta every night. They're in prisoners' jail all right – trying to tunnel out, banging their heads on the walls. Not us. Red flag or black – we give the kids real bling, the girls can have fiancés with a bit of cash, even a Merc—'

I say, 'But you're the philosopher, the little king – it doesn't have a cash price.'

He says, 'Well, I settle for that,' smugly.

Things are happening. The underground is filling up – the Romanians have gone, gilders are working on the marble, the Mercedes are junked, and Edsels and Chargers take their place – some garden statues, maybe by Praxiteles or maybe not, but anyway dredged up, corroded finely, and beneath the underneath there's Chinese jewellers copying stuff, and we are all upmarket, and the guys who come to view wear sharkskin suits, and bodyguards and Raybans, and they pay in cash.

Vast projects are afoot. The point is now – to change the world. Enough understanding it!

Marco is exalted! 'Buried treasure,' he shouts. 'Come and find it!'

Huge pits are dug. The earth moves. The periphery vanishes beneath piles of sod. The sewage, released, stinks. The underground becomes an Elevated. We are like a true Naples, as we should be, volcanoed, buried in our subsoil. Tepid, smelly, swarming with diggers, steel and human. Everyone's employed – not a shovel stays on sale, the houses crack and yaw, the cars becalmed. It is a heavenly pause in a land of hell. The theatre shakes, it's all too big for rhetoric.

'What the devil?' I ask Marco.

'We're burying our treasures! All this stuff – who knows who put it here – the temples, colossuses, the places where the rhinos died, and ostriches beheaded – delicate stuff, you realise – all that, Romans, Greeks, Phoenicians, Persians, Kushans too, I wouldn't wonder and the guys from Arakan, sounds like a musical but it wasn't—' and he roars like a volcano at its moment of ejaculation. 'Then the museums, galleries, the guys in uniforms, the experts that you never see, platoons of wild dogs among the ruins – that's our treasure. All dug up. Gloated over.'

'And for tourists, and the critics too – and guys with little badger brushes, cataloguing and that,' I add.

He is in spate. 'But you see – it's all dug up – for what? The gods and goddesses are gone, they'll never be returning – the nymphs that lived in laurels, those little stands of bamboo – all gone down, cemented over, the tombs defiled or carried off, the sacrificial animals without a tomb, a cross, a turban – nothing to recall those torrid afternoons of blood and booze,' and he pauses.

I see he's shouting at the Superintendent of Treasures, small, bearded guy – he that would keep our treasures visible.

And Marco says, 'Look at the value these old things are sitting on! The prime sites, shopping malls and parks for kiddies, covered with this useless antique worn-out stuff, the blocks laid down by titans, water engineering – secrets all gone to purgatory, – never be restored,' and he rants on. The Superintendent now is nodding, now he looks like puking, but he's torn between his interest and his interests.

Marco concludes. 'We're burying it all. Maybe some day, they'll dig it up again. And put it in the city centres – maybe the universities will pay. But for the while, we'll lay them back – from glass cases to the alabaster dogbirds, from embalmed accountant to the beautiful lady mummies with their bones all poking through. Back to the earth.'

The Superintendent says feebly, 'Tourists?'

Marco shouts, 'Shopping! That's what they want. And gawping at the poor. And maybe having their fat pockets picked. But shopping – that's what they do, that's what they want, and we will give it to them – no more boredom, picky steps around some goddam wall or peering at some squashed jewels or corpses. Who wants that on holiday? And you,' he snarls at the Superintendent, 'You, with your complaints – cement and speculation, vandalism, ignorance – we'll solve your problems for you! Pack it all away. And if the Yanks decide to send another army – this time they won't loot the lot – we'll lay out parking for them for their tanks, and if it's them or Chinese or Indians, whoever has the heaviest armour – we'll save these treasures, safely deep. Occupying armies? They won't spoil a thing. Our past can sleep – safe at last. No dog will dig it up again, sharp claws or not.'

And I think – lots of cash in the shopping centres.

And Marco adds, 'And everyone is making bread – I mean, by digging. Bury this old crap, and build the new. Maybe give everyone a job, that would be a fine idea, when you're making cities. Sticking in the architecture, tax offices, bus stops, all that stuff. Something to do! What a fine notion!'

He is illuminated, he is savant, Peter the Great and Constantine. Burier of the awful, the sweet, the stinking, city, bringer of death and bronchitis. Its absent gods, its load of burials.

The burial of the superfluous city took several weeks. Then we settled down. The Bright Stars were not mentioned, the media placed the praise and blame on politicians, and I saw Marco, concerned citizen, speaking on TV for both pros and cons. He said to me, 'Old Hegel said "everything has its argument" and of course he's right.'

*

A new campaign is started, Marco calls it 'universal people'.

'You see, there's quite a lot of figures who are recognised by name across the world. In Italy, for instance, there's a Romeo and Juliet house, and people come to stare. Now, you take Gandhi and Jesus Christ, Hitler and Buddha, Stalin and Beethoven and Chaplin and Monroe, and lots of heroines and heroes still among us – and we'll consecrate to each a spot. Take Engels's

Leap, for instance – on the cliff, restrained by old Karl Marx – a marvellous scene. And you should know – at school you did that stuff,' and wearily I say,

'No, not me, I wasn't there – it's just the Serbian name I bear, but not the history, and anyway, it all slid off the backs of those who had to listen. Besides, it was Engels had his ashes tossed off Beachy Head, and Marx was dead, and neither of them suicidal,' but Marco carries on,

'Well, what you want? Authenticity? You know, the Yanks have spread throughout the world – places of pilgrimage for creatures who never did, who can't, exist – Mickey and Minnie – find them everywhere. And novelists – now there's a thing! You take your *War and Peace* – the battles that there really were, the people that there really weren't. Where's your reality factor? Or take your *Lady with the Little Dog* – a bit more specialised here – but ladies and their dogs, big ones as well – and who is there doesn't have a favourite dog? We'll have them walking up and down, and maybe they'll want to turn a trick or two, they have apartments ready, and they chain the dog outside, unless of course ...' and he winks slyly.

I say, 'There's no end to it. If you run short, invent a few more places and characters, and in the people go, movies and songs as well – a to and fro of people, as the money circulates, the millions come – the least familiar characters will be the most exotic – nomadism on immense scales, all in the name of culture.'

He takes me up, and gallops on, 'Yes, and you'll find that character begets more characters, more popularity – the best, the worst, saint and murderer, the singer out of tune, blind sword-swallowers, the paraplegic organist – you're right: there is no end. It is another treasure, and we'll build it all!'

'We?' I ask.

'Our affiliates.'

'It seems to me you soon will run the world, at least its wealth resources.'

'Slowly, slowly,' he says. 'Too much success can put you in the frame. The target.'

*

The plans all take some days to realise, but everyone is keen, they work as if they're making millions, but the daily rate goes down and down, and Marco says,

'That's classical economics for you – got to respect the classics,' and he says to me, 'I've got a plan for Bic and Johnny. What do rich kids want to do, since reading, writing, stuff at school, it grinds you down, and what's the fun, and what's the point? They want to hang out on the street, and maybe drink and smoke a little, stuff like that, and maybe play some pool and kick a ball around.'

I anticipate him. 'Sport in schools?'

'Old stuff. No, only sport – the only subject. Makes a lot of cash – no trouble now for poor and stupid guys – they understand what being good at games entails, it's sinking balls and netting them. And since they're amateurs, a little booze and smoke – that does no harm – you maybe give the concession to the school, a little bar, and one of ours to sell them junk to snort and smoke. And for those places where they don't have teachers – sports agents, managers! – they'll do the job, the cash comes in by selling guys to play in richer parts. And everyone is happy. On the street or on the field – see, there's no distinction, no distinction too of class or colour, all that crap, the ones that kick those balls the best will reach the top, and even make it to be – one of our "eternal people". Now, true, I can't yet think of any athlete's names, but that's because I'm just ideas – that, and my comrades' welfare. But, in one move, I've solved the problem both of poverty and school – both, until now, two dull experiences. Maybe one day I'll do the same for all unsightly groups that don't fit in our tourist round – those malcontents who don't throw their culture in the universal hat and want to keep it to themselves. There'll be an answer too, that isn't just to kill or jail them all. I'm working on it – trouble is, the cash incentive isn't there,' and he looks sad and thoughtful.

*

I think of Elektra as – electric blonde. And Katya was dark as a mulberry. Elektra passing from Dan, perhaps to Bic, and now to Johnny. An awkward family history, matricide and incest – who'd call their child like that, Elektra, unless they were just ignorant.

Can't say much for me, spy, at best observer. That's what they call the spies until they catch them. But Igor's the betrayer – first betraying me, that's quite banal. But then, betraying Katya. To the Bright Stars, or doing it all herself.

Elektra's quite a wit – I hear her tell a joke to Johnny. 'There was this cat, and a guy who loved her, to distraction, really. And she went missing, missing for a week and he was crying every day, his life scooped out, and wondering where the hell she'd gone and why, what, where. And the cat meets another cat who asks her what she's doing wandering about, she says, 'People – they come and go, you can't rely on them.'

And she laughs long, and Johnny stares and says it isn't funny, not a bit.

Katya, the cat. Katya.

*

Igor says, 'I'm not Russian, so I can forget the Chechens.'

I say, 'I have no country. We both have fake names, which indicate nothing except history, a dark future for yours, no future for mine. Yet I remember the Chechens, and those who died with them. What more can I do?'

'You can give me a hand with *Romeo and Juliet*,' says Igor.

'What's the angle?' Bic – Laptop – asks.

'It's about gangs,' says Igor.

I say, 'Then let's not do it.'

Igor explains, 'Two kids get their orders crossed, then – friendly fire.'

Dan guesses all the details: 'Let the girls do it. We guys won't. Besides, they're part of it.'

Igor says, 'That way it's not dramatic.'

We discuss what might be dramatic, but nothing improves on our daily lives.

Dan says, 'Well, Elektra's got all her family stuff to happen. Lots of vendetta there.'

Laptop muses, 'It's not personal, just the way you get to live,' and Dan agrees, 'Just relations, everybody's got them. Even whole countries.'

We all agree.

Dan says, 'Elektra can do the play. It's if she wants,' and adds, 'Johnny likes young flesh. The loyalty.'

Giulietta says, 'At that age, my age, tastes are not set firm,' and Franca says – she to be Romeo – 'I hope mine never are. What I don't see in this, is where's the tragedy? Did the author guy get tired of writing? Was it a piece against the gangs, or parents? For us, the gangs sustain, a code ...'

And Giulietta says, 'Like monks. Or nuns. But cleaner,' then they both commiserate with poor Elektra – 'They say she lost her mother, then her brother went all odd – she keeps herself confined within her jokes. She's really comic, but inside she's sad,' and Igor says,

'Who isn't? That's the great alibi – that what you see is what you get, and what you want, although somewhere hidden there is something else, twice as desirable but too good for you, you superficials clinging to our surfaces,' and it's true, you'd better not scratch off the paint, below you'll find the raw stuff, ruins, restorers' stucco.

'Well,' says Igor, are you ready for the play?'

Franca says, 'If I'm half of Romeo, I'd like to be the brash, the pretentious bit, it's easier than the depths,' and Igor says,

'There isn't any depth around, just poetry, the whole goddam theatre trade is made of potboilers, some well wrought – but in the end ... And maybe he should have stuck with a real tale of vengeance sought and suicide and states that kill – but after all, what changes? No one believes that stuff.' And Igor with his clangs and bangs can't change a thing, though better so, for if he was an active man, he'd rant us all to silence.

And Giulietta says, 'I'll do the role, if then I can have Bic.'

Igor says, 'What the hell condition is that?' And she says, 'Well, the Bright Stars are my family – brothers and cousins here. And I choose Bic, the clever, or at least the skilful, one. The least demanding,' and Igor spits and fumes, but has no promises to give, and Giulietta says 'no deal'.

Marco is worried, 'Success brings trouble. We're not brigands, you can't just sweep us away. Maybe we should be a little state. Lots of miniatures around, I'm sure our passports will go well. I think we'll offer first a few thousand, discounted, then a hundred thou, full price. Protection and no taxes, just a help in business, and a flag. We'll find a good big country to be nice to us – I think China – Russia has its hands full – somehow we'll make out.'

I ask, 'A flag with skull and crossbones?' and he laughs,

'That's a part of it. Easier a state than found a religion, though I'd thought of that. The trouble with a new religion is there's no room left – and no returns. Promises of paradise – you can't propose that again, and what then is there left? Meditation you can do at home, we'll bill you for the CD disc and carpet. Now, with Igor's help, we have an epic – the three Juliets, tragically cut short, but winning the sympathy of every teen, and feminism as our creed. And every kind of bandit wants to be ambassador – embassy mail that's snoop-free, and the palace – invited guests, and no one else.' He's quite poetic.

'You'll just go down the path again,' I say, 'some guys get voted in, or just show up, they'll make the rules and kick you out – before you've breathed, you'll be on trial, the mail is searched – and then you'll find the gangs have filtered in and off we go again. History. Law. State.' He says, 'By then I'll be long gone. Eternal return, it doesn't bother me – you know it comes, you just keep running.'

'Territory, Marco,' I say, 'You need some of that.'

'The theatre, the welcome centre down below – and then below all that, the temples, stores, the catacombs, rivers and caverns, stuff you've never seen. And for the military stuff – we've got the red tank!'

He digs deeper in his fantasy, 'Think of the Vatican – just a basilica and a post office. A state won't protect us, but it gives a chance when you must fight. It can give the lost boys something to look up to,' though he smiles wistfully. 'Medals, deaths in action, and parades. Lots of parades, with bands and acrobats, and prelates. 'Bags of swank', like they say in the army. Stomping up and down. A zoo – important that, a hippo, tunnels of love, and candy floss, some apes. Remember all those plays they used to have – the wildest details, actresses in Greek boots, herds of invisible rhinos dashing through, the tramps, the scenes in hell – and not to mention operas. Now it's all gone, the literalness, the real all fantasised – and now it's up to Igor and his fiddling. And we shall see it once again, all culture put together, common language, all that stuff. The Bright Stars' state – a skull, for sure, that's on the flag – but then we'll put some bright stars too – a kind of tinsel, shining and now and then a twinkling. Constant and true. An anthem – maybe some sweet rock, or – dare we try a blues? We saunter down the avenues, as cool as cool, and take a bock, under the lime trees, forever seventeen,' and he is far away.

'The lost boys?' I ask.

'Stay lost, I fear,' he says. 'But they shall have a flag to wrap around. Dead in action! No more philosophy, but – "dead on the field of honour". Makes the blood run hot.' He is fulfilled already, a patriot of one, his head, sliced at the neck, on coins of white recycled metal. It is beautiful. It is terrible.

*

Igor is angry. 'They won't see my play as their blood myth. The sex scenes would have pulled the crowds.'

'The Bright Stars maybe don't deserve you,' I say.

'You and I, we scan the broader scene,' he says, the kindest thing he's said since he made Katya a betrayer, before perhaps she went on to betray him.

He says, 'Marco, our Mercutio. Says being killed's bad luck, so he won't play.'

But Marco says he's master of two worlds, order below, chaos above. 'I hoped – I hope – to make a paradise – horses, rebirth. I fancy myself a hero, mounted, armoured.'

Something rests still in my memory, something he'll not escape, will carry with him. His justice can be very rough indeed, and though his city moves, it's mostly buried, sporting, shopping – what will become of it?

*

Then, we hear that Johnny's dead. And there he is, a little broken envelope, left there on the threshold, so small, the smallest of the Stars, and dead, leaving only some black hole. The Stars come running – there's no mark on him, but he has fixed the public works – the burying, conversion of the schools, and all those malls, some buried too, and some reared up like plate glass hills.

There is a ceremony newly invented. They'll wall him

up, just as he is, his Raybans droop, they jam the glasses back but he's not looking – the anthem isn't ready, as they can't decide, one faction is for Mahler, the other favours 'Jellyrolls' – and here's Elektra. We all keep well back, for grief can be a plague, but she's quite quiet, a Star was born and now is fallen, and she tries some tunes, and in the end we have a wobbly 'Che sarà, sarà'.

They put him in the wall, behind a marble slab that nearly kills its porters as it sways – I see an epitaph, it's been drilled out – no name, no dates, just 'This was one he couldn't fix', a star, a skull. It's very delicate, and for a moment we all stand, are speechless, then thankfully we move away, and jokes are told and someone has a flask, and Johnny's mind is somewhere else, if anywhere at all, and so ours too move off.

Elektra says, 'I'll have to move back with my mother, will she be wild!'

'Her' Johnny. Lover. Cousin? Brother?

Igor mutters, 'Well, all the play's a bit of rant, a teen-age stabbing, and to cut things short – dealing with grief leads to a suicide – now we've discovered moving on, but that would take too long to show and anyway,' he pauses and confides, 'It lacks a bit of zip.'

I'm sure we're sorry for old John, but circumstances being what they are, it's best to wipe him out – an epitaph is better than an autopsy, revenge is quite another mode, and in the end, who cares if some young warrior, thug, is made to pay for Johnny's death – the payment in this case. It can't be cashed. But Marco has the leader's touch, he says,

'We'll take the red tank out!'

He and I examine it. It is very red. Even the tracks are partly red. Marco says, 'There must be ways to make it spew red smoke.'

We fiddle with the tank. It's full of beastly stuff inside, for killing blind, and Marco says – 'Maybe we'll find a driver in the basement here,' and off he goes, a brain on legs – his Mandarin is coming well, again I think how fine a mind he has, and he perhaps can read the thought, he says, 'Well, Johnny could fix things when I told him to – at least I didn't bomb warriors on camels,' and he adds, as if he's only now aware,

'I'm off. I'm leaving. Igor will have to find his Big Idea all by himself.'

I'm amazed, I say, 'But it's all yours, this city.'

'It's rubbish!' he says. 'This state, flawed at its birth – as they all are – some ideal is lacking here. The pretty part is buried, all the rest is shopping and illliterates. How'll they read my poetry?'

I am observer only, but the brain and soul of all this splendid modern ruin – it is his, is Marco's. I ask,

'How could the kids read their computer screens anyway,' and he brightens.

'We cut it down to symbols, like when you drive a car – just things to push and little picture signs. But poetry is different', and although I'm glad he didn't make me read it – me being businessman and manager, on it had gone to Igor, who had stacks of stuff awaiting judgement – like an appeals court judge. Then he says,

'I'm off to look for Katya.'

And I'm even more amazed. 'What would you do when you found her?'

He says, 'Something would occur, singly or together – something we'd improvise. And when I find her, I'll be back.'

I think, oh no, no second coming. I persist, I'd never

thought of looking for a person, now it seems quite smart – 'Where and how, what's the starting point?'

He says, 'Extreme humility – though I exclude the sandal look, the begging bowl, you'd not get far on those. We have affiliates, you know.'

'But here, who'll be the boss?' I say. 'If you're not here, no one outside will understand.'

He must think I'm superficial, for he says, 'Power isn't found just in one knot in the net. The net itself is powerful – it's all one. If I need power to find her – maybe luck's enough – that I can rely on, from the net.'

My mind bubbles with questions. Where? the Cold Mountains? Where do free persons go, is there a country, town, or railway, some parking lot outside a bar where free spirits leave a note of where they've gone, and if you are to know?

He says, 'Humility, and poverty – relative, of course. The places I'd most like to see – they're probably the ones that she'd like most.'

That is true. And Dan and Bic the hacker now are all that's left, the state is up and gasping – time to move on. This state is born of blood, as they all are – we'll stick the law and morals on like plaster on a wound. And maybe Marco will find Katya, and her tragedy. Elektra is sad, sad to return to Mother, but Katya is a beast who's left her cage and wanders waterless and desperate – it is right that Marco, warrior, poet, murderer, should start his quest now that his friend is dead. 'The best fixer a man could want,' says Marco.

The splendid entrance to the basement. The bronze doors open, and the tank trundles out – only black fumes, though Marco did his best to make them red. The tracks are squealing like two boars in heat. It seems the committee couldn't reach agreement, and behind the Mahler I hear Jellyrolls.

Those doors will never close again, and off the tank goes, round and round the city – and soon there's little kids on top and some end up beneath the tracks and Dan can't stop the juggernaut, maybe he doesn't want to as it's firing now – they must be blanks, they say that every good revolution starts with firing blanks, but I'd don't see a revolution here. And now some guys are firing back, and some are cheering as they shoot, and round it goes – I see that on the flag there's Marco's head, with Katya's entwined, and so we're for the family, in some way – though whether Katya is in a place where she can be found, I've some doubts, and Marco's search – it may be epic but in fact he either knows, or else the search is fruitless.

And here's Elektra and her mother. What does it all mean, the sadness, family, mother, child? I hardly want to hear. Destiny, choice – what cons!

I think the girl is pregnant. She's just stopped painting, no more culture, maybe no more sadness and hysteria, the mother's safe, perhaps it's our success. That's it, the end.

'Not the real Elektra, then,' I say.

'What do you mean, real,' she's angry – her last trick, designed some coins, the new state bears the head of Marco, neatly decapitated. It all seems silly, this revenge and matricide and teenage love – all meaningless, hurting in one place, taking it out quite randomly on someone else. And if another Johnny's born, he won't be here alone, and though I'd like to say a Star is born, or will be, all we can see is how a state is roaring into being.

It's irresistible, or at least it is for me, I'm tired of

being Mr Zero and maybe I let out a scream or two, and Igor is quite wild with joy and rage and signs himself repeatedly – maybe a cross or could be anything, but now our tricky origins are quite submerged. Whatever it will be is rising from the ash, a monument of ash itself, at least they're building something – place that was horrible at the start is now quite decorous, with marble, tombs and stuff.

It must be Laptop firing, and he's found a new vocation – from reason into action in a moment – makes the gun traverse from plain to mall, and now he's picking off the marksmen with the tank's machine gun, and already there's processions starting, dead in open coffins, as is right. The restaurants are overbooked, the tears are running out and everyone is angry, but without another tank there's little they can do, the gangs are running short of men and ammunition, and it seems our side has won – there's only two Stars left, but who's to know – somewhere in China and entombed behind the walls there's another couple – heroes, heroines, even poems and an anthem.

I fancy we shall do a play, and everyone will show, Elektra and her kid, and Johnny's ghost and all the bosses and affiliates, all patriots for the evening, maybe a calmer flag – with Marco and his bride, whoever he has found, passing her off as Katya – the founder, shaper – triumphantly returned. And they'll all celebrate, the booze is free, the pistols checked out at the door, and we shall all be one.

And there will be a special happening, in solemn procession, giving thanks, we'll say: 'Today is history, today is ours. Today is Red Tank Day.'

About the author

John Fraser has lived in Rome since 1980. Previously, he worked in England and Canada.

www.ingramcontent.com/pod-product-compliance
Lightning Source LLC
Chambersburg PA
CBHW020551310726
48979CB00008B/1168/J

* 9 7 8 0 9 5 6 1 4 0 9 4 4 *